BOOK FOUR
THE SUMMER OF MAGIC QUARTET

BEHIND THE
SORCERER'S CLOAK

ANDREA SPALDING

ORCA BOOK PUBLISHERS

Library and Archives Canada Cataloguing in Publication

Spalding, Andrea

Behind the sorcerer's cloak / Andrea Spalding.
(The summer of magic quartet ; bk. 4)

ISBN 1-55143-627-2

I. Title. II. Series: Spalding, Andrea. Summer of magic quartet; bk. 4.

PS8587.P213B43 2006   jC813'.54
C2006-903256-4

First published in the United States, 2006
Library of Congress Control Number: 2006928467

Summary: In Book Four of *The Summer of Magic Quartet*, the Dark Being is poised to
conquer Earth and after that, the Universe. Only the four Magic Children can restore the
balance between Light and Dark.

Orca Book Publishers gratefully acknowledges the support for its publishing programs
provided by the following agencies: the Government of Canada through the Book Publishing
Industry Development Program and the Canada Council for the Arts, and the Province of
British Columbia through the BC Arts Council and the Book Publishing Tax Credit.

Orca Book Publishers
PO Box 5626, Station B
Victoria, BC Canada
V8R 6S4

Orca Book Publishers
PO Box 468
Custer, WA USA
98240-0468

Cover and interior images by Martin Springett
Typeset and design by Christine Toller

www.orcabook.com
Printed and bound in Canada

09 08 07 06 • 5 4 3 2 1

For Graham and Nina, whose friendship has spanned my lifetime.

Thank you for sharing the mystical places of Mann.

Andrea Spalding

A talisman to hone the mind,
A circlet old to hold and bind,
A staff to smite with hidden might,
Beads to link and hold the light.

Note: In the text I use the following as a spell: *Manannan Beg Mac y Leir Mie goll magh as ny share goll stiagh.* This line translates as "Manannan Beg Mac y Leir, give safe journey out and a better journey home." These words are the first two lines of the traditional Manx Fisherman's prayer asking Manannan for a safe sea journey. The translation by Fenella Bazin is found in her book *Ree ny Marrey: Songs of the Isle of Man* and used with permission.

TABLE OF CONTENTS

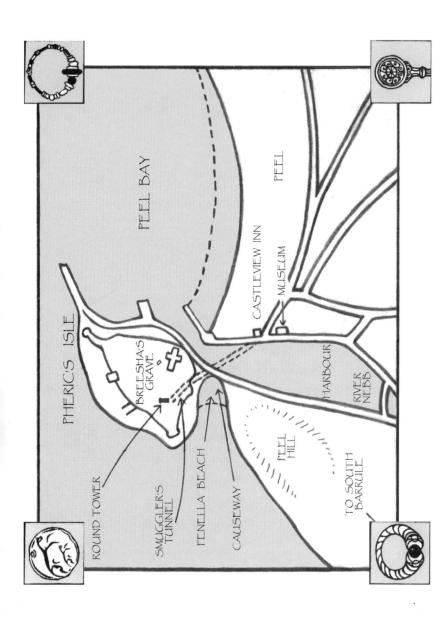

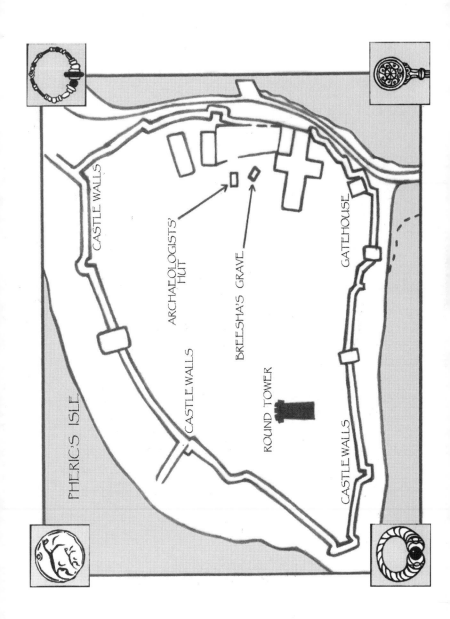

PHERIC'S ISLE

CASTLE WALLS

CASTLE WALLS

CASTLE WALLS

CASTLE WALLS

ARCHAEOLOGISTS' HUT

BREESHA'S GRAVE

ROUND TOWER

GATEHOUSE

CHAPTER ONE

A Stirring in the Mists of Time

Sinister disturbances roused the sorcerer Manannan from sleep.

He tilted his head to listen.

Ripples of sound echoed through the Mists of Time. He must heed them. Manannan shook off sleep and stumbled to the summit of his mountain home, South Barrule.

Night mist billowed around him, cloaking, blanketing. It concealed the view. Mist was his to command. He was its Keeper. In return the mist was his cloak of safety, the means by which he hid his island kingdom from unfriendly eyes. Manannan spread wide his arms and slowly raised them.

The mist obeyed his command. It swirled and lifted, though tendrils teased him by covering his eyes.

Manannan chuckled and brushed them away. "I am the Sorcerer Manannan. I am found in the mist and the rain, and you must answer to me." The threads dissolved and the Island of Mann spread below, washed in the clear starlight of pre-dawn.

It was a small kingdom for such a powerful mage. From his heather-clad mountain, almost the entire island could be seen. But size was of no account. Here worlds met. Magic and humans lived side by side. Manannan's kingdom was the center of Earth Magic: the place chosen by the Sleeper.

Manannan's eyes raked the scene.

Everything slept.

Manannan turned his attention to the magical heart of his kingdom, the castle on tiny Pheric's Isle lying off his western shore.

Starlight threw the ruined castle walls into sharp relief. They surrounded the tiny isle like a curtain, protecting the tall Round Tower rising in the center.

Nothing stirred.

Manannan probed deep into the heart of the Round Tower. There, layer upon layer of magic webbed around secrets forgotten by humans.

He relaxed. The webs of magic on Pheric's Isle remained intact. Both Tower and Sleeper slept undisturbed.

Manannan bowed to the universe in a gesture of thanks.

Whatever the disturbance in the Mists of Time, all seemed well on Mann.

He was mistaken. The ripples had roused the Moddy Dhoo.

The feared Black Dog lay awake beneath the castle gatehouse. Its red eyes pierced the darkness. The Moddy

Dhoo sensed what Manannan couldn't. The Sleeper was under threat.

⁂

The new day dawned, but all was not well across the Irish Sea in the city of Glastonbury, in the heart of England.

Three children were trying not to panic.

Seven-year-old Chantel struggled with tears. Her brother, Adam, was missing.

"What are we going to do? How can we get Adam back when we don't even know where he is?" Chantel's voice shook. Fresh tears trickled down her cheeks as she looked up at the glum faces of her two older cousins. "We can't ask anyone for help. N-no one will believe he's vanished through a magic portal." She dropped the piece of toast she was holding and buried her head in her hands.

Her cousins, Holly and Owen, looked for support across the breakfast table. Their friend and neighbor, Mr. Smythe, was the only adult who knew of their adventures.

Mr. Smythe looked drawn and gray. He shrugged helplessly as he patted Chantel's shoulder.

"This Magic is beyond me. I—I don't know how to help. Our best plan is to wait for the Wise Ones. Trust that Myrddin will bring Adam back."

"That's what we're doing," said Owen bitterly. "But it's taking forever."

⁂

Three times Holly and Owen and their Canadian cousins Chantel and Adam had helped Myrddin and two other magical beings, the Wise Ones, outwit a shadowy figure known as the Dark Being.

The first two adventures had been successful.

Chantel had helped Equus, the Great White Horse, find his talisman.

Owen had helped Ava, the spectacular Hawkwoman, regain her circlet.

The third adventure, when Adam was to help Myrddin regain his staff, had ended in disaster.

"Everything started so well," moaned Holly. "Adam was brilliant at finding his way through the Spiral Labyrinth and unlocking the entrance into Glastonbury Tor."

"And it was Adam who released Myrddin's staff from its hiding place in the Crystal Cave," agreed Owen. "He was fantastic. If only he'd not grabbed Zorianna's cloak when she pinched the staff from Myrddin. That was really daft."

"No, it wasn't," said Chantel, bristling. "Adam was brave. Really brave. I'd like to see you standing up to the Dark Being's emissary." She gave a sob. "I just wish he'd let go before they vanished through a portal."

It was all so overwhelming Chantel could hardly bear to think about it.

Owen pushed his plate away. "Our adventures were fun at first. Now they're scary."

"Come off it. There was always a scary side," said Holly. Her voice was determinedly matter of fact. "But they always ended okay. Don't you dare give up. This adventure will end okay too. Adam will be found. Myrddin's gone to rescue him." Despite her resolve, her voice wobbled at the end. She too watched the sky and ignored her food.

Owen thrust his chair back. "I don't get it. Where are the other Wise Ones? Ava and Equus said to call if we needed them. We do. We called ages ago." He stalked across the room, yanked the French doors open and stepped outside onto the patio.

"Come on, Ava. Come on, Equus," he whispered.

"Oh, do shut up," said Holly quietly, from behind him. "That's the hundredth time already. You're making everything worse."

"Well, why aren't they here?" snapped Owen. "Know what? I think something bad's happened." He challenged Holly. "You think so too, don't you?"

Holly flushed and jerked her head toward Chantel who was joining them.

It was too late.

Chantel burst into fresh tears and fled upstairs. The bedroom door slammed.

Mr. Smythe glared at Owen and followed her.

"Idiot," said Holly. She slumped on the nearest wooden chair. "Chantel can't take any more. She's only seven. How would you feel if I'd disappeared?"

The hint of a grin tugged at the corner of Owen's mouth.

Holly gave him a little push. "No...don't bother to answer! Learn some tact."

Owen flopped into a patio chair beside her. "I didn't mean to upset Chantel, or Mr. Smythe, but we've got to face it, Holly. Something's wrong."

Holly grimaced.

"Come on, Holly. Admit it." Owen thumped the table

between them. "The Wise Ones are in trouble! I bet the Dark Being's got them!"

Holly stopped him again. "Don't even think that way," she said fiercely. "We've got to keep light in our hearts. They said so."

"All right, all right." Owen shrugged. "So she hasn't got them. I'm keeping light in my heart. Now what?"

"Wait and hope," said Holly firmly.

Owen slumped. "I'm fed up with waiting. I wish we weren't just kids."

"What difference would that make? Mr. Smythe's an adult, and he hasn't a clue."

"Well, something better happen soon. We go home tomorrow. We've gotta get Adam back," said Owen.

They sat in silence, trying not to think the unthinkable.

***

Adam clung to the hem of Zorianna's cloak as she dragged him through the Mists of Time.

His eyes were scrunched shut. His hands gripped the fabric with fingers of steel.

He was terrified. He knew they were going to Zorianna's mistress, the Dark Being.

This is the dumbest thing I've ever done, he thought bitterly. But no way was he going to let go. No way was he going to let Zorianna steal the staff he'd worked so hard to get.

Zorianna sped up.

Adam groaned.

***

Among the stars, evil smirked.

"I found it!" crowed the Dark Being to her servant. She stared down at a small blue planet. "Insignificant Gaia, the place the humans call Earth. This is where the Tools of Power are hidden." She chuckled. "The Wise Ones could not conceal their traces forever. The planet tingles with their magic."

She studied the magical trail left by the Wise Ones, and her anger, always close to the surface, began to rise. "The Wise Ones know I have approached, yet they feel hope, not despair. Why? Old Magic will do them no good. I will prevail. I am the most powerful being in the universe." She shook out her tumble of dark curls, lifted her face to rejoice in the darkness around her and stretched out her arms to the universe.

The large jet-black stone on the ring around her third finger glowed darkly. She looked at it and smiled as she rubbed the stone in a circular motion. "Darkness will triumph! My power grows as each day passes. My army has grown to millions, and my enemies are but four beings who gave up their Tools of Power." She laughed. "How can the Wise Ones stop me? Soon the entire universe will understand the beauty of Darkness."

She sent out a trumpet call of mindspeak to her Shades and emissaries searching the nearby stars.

Return, my emissaries. Come, come, come, my Shades. The hiding place of the Tools of Power has been discovered. Zorianna has descended to retrieve them. Gather so we can celebrate and witness the final fading of the Wise Ones.

The Dark Being stared down at Gaia again. Her lips

twitched. "What a ridiculous hiding place! What were the Wise Ones thinking? Earth Magic is pitifully simple and Old Magic almost forgotten. Neither can ever match my magic. Already I am more powerful than individual Wise Ones. With even one tool I can destroy Equus, Ava and Myrddin. Then I can overcome the Lady and take the necklace."

She laughed, savoring the thought of victory, then shouted in mindspeak through time and space. *Hurry, Zorianna. You are the greatest of my emissaries. Find the Tools quickly. Bring them, and we shall celebrate everlasting Darkness. I will reward you well.*

Full of good humor, the Dark Being settled down to wait. She used the time to consider her next move. How should she best reward her loyal army of Shades? Should she entertain them by destroying Gaia? Complete annihilation was exciting and satisfying to watch. It would cement their belief in her power, though they had seen her destroy many planets before.

No, something different was called for this time.

What if she sent the Shades themselves down to Gaia? Yes. She would let them terrorize the humans and create a new race of Darklings to serve both themselves and her.

Below, the small blue planet humans called Earth spun on through the Mists of Time.

Holly, short of sleep from the night's activities, could no longer keep her eyes open. She cushioned her head on her arms at the patio table and dozed. Her mind fluttered in and out of a strange dream.

She flew over a silver sea toward a castle, built on a small island. From the castle's center rose a tall round tower, pointing like a finger to the sky.

Holly swooped over the castle walls.

A figure stood on the circular platform at the top of the tower, a cloaked figure wearing a glowing necklace. One arm was outstretched and silver threads of magic spun from the fingers, creating a delicate web of light that spiraled to the stars. The other hand gripped the necklace.

"Who are you?" cried Holly. "Please tell me?" She dove toward the tower.

The figure looked up.

Holly had a flash of recognition; she'd seen those eyes before.

Sea mist blew between them. The tower was gone.

Lost and disoriented, Holly flailed her arms desperately.

"Ouch." Holly woke with a start. She had whacked one arm hard on the chair beside her.

She sat up, rubbing the bruise and wiping the shadows of sleep from her eyes. Faint images from the dream lingered. She tried to recapture them, distressed that she didn't recognize the figure. Then she stretched and yawned, and the dream was gone.

Once again, Holly watched the sky and wished for Adam's safe return.

Loud murmurings in the Mists of Time roused Manannan a second time. He climbed again through the walls and ditches of his fortified mountain, to stand on Barrule's peak, within the horseshoe wall of rocks. He stared deep into the bright morning sky.

He stiffened.

A patch of strange blankness marred the sky. It was as though a cloud hovered, though no cloud was to be seen. Feelings of evil and rage oozed from the place.

He had been warned to watch for this. The cloud that was not a cloud concealed the arrival of the terrible Dark Being. She was here and watching Gaia.

Manannan shut his eyes and probed the edge of the blankness. He shuddered at the hatred he sensed.

He tuned into the Mists again.

The magical Mists of Time hummed with information: Zorianna, an emissary from the Dark Being, had captured Myrddin's staff. A human child was trying to recover it.

Manannan listened with amazement. The Mists of Time had been silent for decades, their magic forgotten by humans. Now they rang with chatter for those who had ears to hear.

Manannan gasped. "This is unbelievable," he said to himself. "A modern child challenging the Dark Being's emissary! No wonder the Mists are alive with talk." He shook his head sadly. "The child has no chance unless it calls upon Old Magic. But modern children do not know about Earth Magic, let alone understand that Old Magic exists. What to do? What to do?"

Manannan cupped his hand to his ear and listened again. The disturbance was growing. Myrddin had entered the Mists to search for the child and his staff.

Despite the gravity of the situation, Manannan smiled. "The Wise One, Myrddin, need not worry about his staff. Its magic is alive and rebelling as it should. The staff will not allow itself to be removed from Gaia by any hand other than his."

Manannan stretched out and caught a few wisps of cloud hanging around Barrule's summit. He pulled the wisps close to his face and whispered. "Go, hum in Myrddin's ear. Tell him the staff and the child approach Mann. Tell him they will find refuge here."

The handful of mist swirled away.

"A pretty kettle of fish indeed." Manannan shook his head. "Mann must be protected and the child saved." He sighed. "First, I must confine the emissary within the magic of Mann, where she can do no harm." He fingered his long white beard. "That may rouse the Sleeper, but perhaps her time has come."

He swiftly plucked more fine strands of sea mist from the air around him and wove them into a ball of thickening magic. He tossed the ball far from Barrule, deep into the Mists of Time.

As the Mists of Time thickened, Manannan cloaked his island with an unseasonable fog. "Out of sight is out of mind," he muttered. "The Dark Being may watch Gaia, but her eye must not alight upon the Kingdom of Mann."

Back in Glastonbury, Holly sat on the patio, waiting for Myrddin. The morning sun was warm, but it gave her no comfort.

Owen returned from prowling the garden.

"How much longer must we wait?" he moaned.

Holly shook her head. She wound a side curl round and round her finger. First one way, then the other.

Like Owen, she was tired of waiting.

In fact she was growing angry.

She'd been waiting all summer! She felt mad just thinking about it.

Her brother and cousins had played key roles in major adventures, and she'd just tagged along. Sure, she had been part of things, but Chantel, Adam and Owen had each been chosen by a Wise One.

She, Holly, had been ignored.

This adventure was supposed to be hers, but now Adam was lost and everything sidetracked. As soon as Adam had found Myrddin's staff, it was supposed to be her turn. She was going to help the mysterious Wise One called the Lady. Now Adam had messed up, and the Lady was silent.

Holly simmered as she looked back over her summer.

Equus the Great White Horse God appeared to Chantel in her dreams. She rode the wind on his back.

Ava, the amazing Hawkwoman, came to Owen in the form of a real hawk as well as in dream form.

Myrddin actually had a human form. They'd all met him, not just Adam. Holly looked around ruefully. This was his home. She was sitting on the patio of Myrddin's house in Glastonbury where he was known as Mr. Green.

So what had happened to the Lady?

Holly's anger rose in a great wave. "Come on, Lady! I'm fed up with being ignored." She kicked the table leg.

"Ouch!" She rubbed her foot and came to her senses.

Owen stared at Holly in amazement. She rarely got angry. What was happening to her?

Holly's flash of anger dissolved. She began to think.

Many things were wrong. Big things. Adam was lost in the Mists of Time; Myrddin had vanished to rescue him. Ava and Equus hadn't come to help. And the Dark Being was approaching.

What if Owen was right and something else was wrong? What if the Lady couldn't contact her?

There could only be one explanation.

"Owen," Holly said slowly. "Old Magic isn't working properly. I think it's spread too thin trying to protect us."

Owen thought for a moment. "You mean it's struggling because so much bad stuff is going on at once?"

"Yes."

"So what? We can't do anything about it."

"Can't we?" Holly let her curl spring back. "We're supposed to be Magic Children."

"So?" said Owen. He shrugged. "None of us has real power. I can't turn you into a frog."

"How do you know?" said Holly.

Owen grinned. "Don't tempt me." He waved an imaginary magic wand. "Abracadabra. Turn Holly into a frog. ...Darn, it didn't work."

"No, seriously. If we are Magic Children we should be doing magic, not just relying on the Wise Ones."

Brother and sister stared at each other.

"Us...do magic on our own? What sort of magic?" said Owen.

Holly suddenly seemed older and more assured, "Think about it. Everything's going wrong because the Dark Being's found Earth. She's affecting how people think and feel. Myrddin said everyone is becoming angry and more warlike. And I did, just now. Anger just swept over me. We need more Earth Magic to counteract the bad stuff, and we are the only humans who can do it."

"Sure, but...but..."

"But nothing. The Wise Ones have been showing us how to use Earth Magic all summer. They told us that humans once used it all the time. We've done it before."

"But only with support," said Owen.

"Not much support. A lot we made up on our own, remember? What did the Stones tell you when we were in Avebury?"

Owen thought for a moment. "That everyone's rituals are different...that earth, air, fire and water are just symbols...it doesn't matter how we use them. That what's important is to concentrate and believe." He looked across at Holly with wide eyes.

"Exactly," said Holly. "So let's do something. Let's concentrate and believe, instead of sitting here. Let's focus on light." Holly grabbed Owen's arm and led the way down the steps to the damp lawn.

<hr>

The Dark Being's chuckle echoed across the universe. Her wait was over. Zorianna was reporting, sending mindspeak and mind pictures of what she'd accomplished on the humans' planet.

Bad news flashed to the stars. *Equus and Ava found their Tools before I reached Gaia, Mistress.*

The Dark Being roared with anger. She paced around, tossing energy bolts and shattering a nearby star.

Eventually she calmed and returned to listen to Zorianna again.

I have more bad news, warned Zorianna. *The Wise Ones have taught four human children about Earth Magic.*

This time the Dark Being snorted in derision. *Four children. What can four human children do against my magic and my army? You are being overly cautious, Zorianna.*

They are no ordinary children, said Zorianna. *They do unexpected things.*

So do I, replied the Dark Being. *Now send me good news.*

Zorianna sent images.

The Dark Being laughed when Zorianna showed how she'd snatched the magic staff from the human child and Myrddin.

She felt the shock wave made by Zorianna thrusting the staff through a portal into the Mists of Time and plunging after it.

A second unexpected shock wave made her gasp, then she laughed again. *So the human boy child followed you, Zorianna? He is grasping the hem of your cloak? What courage! If he survives the journey, that boy shall help me conquer Gaia. He will teach me Earth Magic. Well done, Zorianna.*

The Dark Being applauded the mind pictures. She threw off her cloak of darkness and revealed her presence, surrounded by a circle of gathering Shades.

Come, Zorianna. Come, human boy. She flung open her arms and waited for them to arrive.

And waited, and waited.

Flashes of anger and despair reached her from Zorianna.

Earth Magic was fighting back. The Mists of Time had thickened.

Zorianna, the boy and Myrddin's staff vanished.

The Dark Being's boiling anger made the fabric of the universe quake. How dare Gaia fight her? Annihilation was too swift a punishment for such treachery. Once she had located Zorianna and the staff, she'd send the Shades to torture and enslave Gaia's inhabitants.

The Dark Being stared at the Mists of Time. She was poised, ready to pounce.

⬚⬚⬚

Holly knelt on the grass in Myrddin's garden and gestured Owen to kneel opposite her.

"Copy me," she ordered.

"Bossy Boots," said Owen.

Holly grinned. "Come on. What have you got to lose?"

"My image. We look daft," said Owen.

Holly refused to be sidetracked. "Copy me," she insisted. "I learned this from one of the dancers in Avebury. It's a way to focus thoughts."

Holly placed her hands flat on the grass before her. "Earth support me," she chanted.

She raised her hands above her head. "Air surround me."

She moved her fingertips to touch her temples. "Fire enlighten me."

She raised her hands above her head. "Water cleanse me."

She folded her hands over her heart.

"Come on, Owen, do it with me."

Owen looked around. No one was watching. "Okay, Sis, here goes."

"Don't call me Sis," said Holly automatically. She placed her hands back on the grass.

Owen rolled his eyes but copied her.

"Earth support me," he mumbled. "Air surround me." He stumbled through the unfamiliar actions and words.

"Good. Now we do it over and over and think of Adam and Myrddin. But you've got to believe. Like we did when we called Ava back in the second adventure. Got it? We've got to believe we are sending Adam and Myrddin hope and protection."

"Okay...okay...I've got the idea." Owen placed his palms on the grass again.

"Earth support me.
Air surround me.
Fire enlighten me.
Water cleanse me."

"Earth support me.
Air surround me.
Fire enlighten me.
Water cleanse me."

Brother and sister chanted the words over and over. With each repetition, their voices grew more assured.

The chant rose and fell, was captured by the breeze and wafted far and wide around Gaia.

***

Adam trembled with fear and exhaustion. The Mists of Time were endless. His strength was fading. They were traveling faster and faster. He could feel it in the way thick cold mist slipped past his body. He hated the sensation.

Zorianna yelped.

Adam forced his fingers to grasp a little more cloak, cracked open his eyes and squinted up.

Something had happened, something had changed.

He wished he hadn't looked. He was dangling from the hem of the cloak, swinging to and fro in slow arcs. He shut his eyes again, sick to his stomach.

"I've gotta look. I need to know what's going on." He spoke sternly to himself, forcing his eyes open to look up along the length of Zorianna's body.

He gasped.

"The staff's rebelling. It's taken over."

Instead of Zorianna carrying the staff, it now dragged her along. She stretched out behind it, struggling to hang on, just as he'd struggled to hang onto her.

Hope flickered in Adam's heart. He remembered Myrddin telling him the staff punished people who wrongly wielded it. Yeah, about time it did something, he thought.

He closed his eyes again and focused on holding on.

The pull on his arms was agonizing. He gritted his teeth and wished for the dreadful journey to end.

Zorianna screamed orders at the staff. "Staff...I command you...Heed me...I am your mistress now."

Adam's eyes flew open again.

The angle of their flight changed.

The staff was dragging them down toward Earth.

"Noooo!" screamed Zorianna. "Up...UP to the Dark Being."

She shouted, cursed and railed, but the staff towed them faster and faster downward.

Without warning, Zorianna swung a leg backward, kicking out at Adam. She was trying to get rid of him to lighten her load!

Adam arched his back and swung his body away from Zorianna's flailing foot.

"Be gone, you human pestilence!" she shrieked.

Sheer panic kept him hanging on. And anger. He'd stuck it out this long. No way was he going to give up if the staff was rebelling. Adam tried to ease his cramping fingers.

He risked letting go with one hand. He wound the hem of the cloak around his wrist to relieve the weight. The movement made him spin round and round in space. He grabbed the cloak again with his free hand.

Closing his eyes, Adam sent a desperate burst of mindspeak.

Someone help me! Someone help me! Someone help me!

Warmth and hope crept around him. A faint chant sang in

his ears, comforting him. He couldn't make out the words, but the voices were familiar. The chant eased his panic and added strength to his fingers. It was as though his cousins were beside him, encouraging him, giving him strength.

Manannan cocked an ear. A song rippled around Gaia. Someone was practicing Earth Magic.

What a pleasant change. He'd thought humans had forgotten. He listened again. "Paitchyn's voices," he murmured softly. "Children." He smiled, heartened by the once familiar chant of earth, air, fire and water.

Deep in the secret heart of his kingdom, magic flickered. The Sleeper began to dream.

Zorianna gave up trying to dislodge Adam.

She turned again to the staff, trying to force it to do her bidding.

Adam watched as Zorianna dragged her body, hand over hand, along the staff's length. "Now I have you," she shrieked. She clamped her knees around the staff, riding it like a broomstick, pulling up on its head.

The staff plummeted like a stone, down through the grayness.

Zorianna grimaced and gripped so tightly her hands turned white.

Adam was pulled along behind. He flinched as Zorianna turned a white face toward him.

"Boy, help me!" she screamed.

Adam shook his head.

"Help me!" she shrieked. "We will both be killed."

Adam groaned. She had a point.

He gave a small nod.

Zorianna hauled on her cloak. "Quickly," she gasped as soon as Adam was within her reach. "Add your weight to the back of the staff. Force the head upward."

Adam glared. He didn't want to help. But his arms needed a break, and he didn't want to hit the ground and become scrambled egg.

"Climb on, boy. You will be rewarded."

Yeah, right, thought Adam. He swung one leg over the staff as Zorianna hauled on the back of his T-shirt.

Whoa...Adam felt safer sitting astride. The new position rested his arms. He took a deep breath, and new courage flowed through his veins. The only drawback was having Zorianna so near. He hated her. He couldn't bear to touch her.

Adam shuffled as far back as he could, perching on the very end of the staff, keeping as big a gap as possible between his body and Zorianna's. He concentrated on the magic that surged through the wood. Myrddin's magic. It felt good.

Zorianna shouted and cussed again.

Myrddin's staff refused to alter direction. On and on it dropped.

Zorianna screamed out spell after spell.

At last, the staff stopped falling.

Adam relaxed for a brief moment before the staff bucked like a horse, stood on end and spun rapidly.

Zorianna threw herself full length, gripping with hands, knees, feet and teeth.

Adam jerked to avoid touching her as the staff gave a corkscrew twist. He flew off and cannonballed through the mist.

"Aaaargggghhhh!"

His cry of despair shivered the stars.

The Mists of Time alerted Manannan. He jumped to his feet. "The boy's in trouble."

He grasped leaves of Bollan Bane, crushed them and threw their dust into the Mists of Time.

"Bollan Bane, good Bollan Bane,

Help this child, in Manannan's name."

Adam, dusted with Bollan Bane, hurtled through the thinned and tattered edges of the Mists of Time.

The Bollan Bane conjured a fleeting vision. A white-haired old man stretched out a hand and called, "Remember Earth Magic, paitchey. Remember the Light."

Adam hardly registered the vision or the message. It didn't matter. He was toast. He was cannonballing toward something that made his skin crawl.

Adam yelled, then screamed as a mind-numbing Shade grabbed him and dragged him into a whirling vortex of hatred.

Still screaming, he was sucked through the maelstrom and dropped into a gray silence.

"Hush, hush. You are safe, courageous boy. I have you," said a voice as velvet as midnight, as sweet as honey.

Adam's head and mind hurt. He felt bruised, body and soul. The tortured muscles in his arms shrieked with pain, and his fingers cramped and ached. He groaned, wished he was dead and realized he was still alive. Adam opened his eyes.

A smiling young woman, her face and shoulders framed by an untamed cloud of curly dark hair, leaned over him.

He lay on a soft wrap at her feet.

Despite his pain, Adam's breath caught. She was beautiful, and as she moved her gown rippled like molten silver. She leaned over and dropped another wrap of exquisite softness over him. She made stroking movements in the air above his body, and the pain dulled.

Relief and gratitude swept over Adam. He'd been rescued. This amazing woman had snatched him from the terror of the Dark Being. His eyes closed. He was so exhausted he couldn't think clearly, but he tried to lift his head to thank her.

A new wave of agony hit. He whimpered and fell back.

He felt the woman gently touch his temples, then stroke his arms and shoulders. The pain began to recede.

Adam tried again.

"Th...thank...you. Thanks...for rescuing me." He shuddered. "The...the dark...the cold...was awful." He struggled to make sense of things. "Are you th...the Lady? Holly said you'd be beautiful." He fought the waves of exhaustion engulfing him. "I...I...thought...the Dark Being had me." He tried to grasp her hand, but muscles spasmed, and his arm fell back. "Th...th...thanks...I'm Adam...a...Magic Child."

·The beautiful young woman smiled and tucked his arm inside the wrap. "Don't try to speak, you're hurt and tired. Sleep, Adam the Courageous, sleep and heal."

Adam's eyes closed. He sank into oblivion.

CHAPTER TWO

STIRRINGS OF EARTH MAGIC

In the hallway of Mr. Green's house in Glastonbury, the phone rang.

Mr. Smythe pounded downstairs as Holly and Owen leapt up and rushed in from the patio. The three collided in the hall.

Holly reached the receiver first. "Hello."

"Good morning, Love. Having fun at the Glastonbury festival? Sorry to phone so early, but we thought you might be out if we left it much later."

Holly lowered the receiver, clamped her hand over the mouthpiece and hissed, "It's Mum. For us!" A wave of longing for the family farm at Uffington and a dose of her mother's good sense swept over her. If only she could confide in her mother.

Holly pushed the thoughts aside, lifted the receiver to her ear again and beckoned Owen.

Owen held his head close so he could hear.

"Glad you answered, Holly," said her mother. "I thought you should know that Chantel and Adam's mother will be phoning from Canada. She called here earlier. I tried to talk her out of contacting you while you were on holiday, but she insists on speaking to Chantel and Adam. I asked her to wait until nine o'clock our time. Then you were all likely to be awake. She's still up, though it's nearly one in the morning in Canada. She's in a state and can't sleep."

Owen lifted his watch and showed it to Holly. It was a quarter to nine.

"I thought Adam and Chantel should be prepared," Lynne, Holly's mother continued. "They were so upset after their mother's last phone call. And with you being away...I'm concerned..." Lynne's voice trailed off.

Holly's brain was working overtime. She mustn't let slip what was happening. "It's okay, Mum. Thanks for the warning. I'll tell Chantel and Adam."

"Maybe I should talk to them?" Lynne said, her voice worried.

"Er...It's okay, Mum. We'll phone you back if there's a problem," said Holly, thinking fast. "Chantel's still up in her bedroom, and...and Adam...Adam has...er...just gone out with Myr...with Mr. Green."

Mr. Smythe gestured at Holly. He mimed using the phone.

Holly nodded at him. "Mr. Smythe's here, Mum. He'd like a word." She handed over the receiver with a sigh of relief.

"That was awful. I was lying to Mum," she whispered to Owen.

"What choice did you have?" Owen whispered back.

"Greetings, Lynne," Mr. Smythe's voice was hearty. "I hope you're not worried about us."

Holly and Owen watched with fascination. They had not realized Mr. Smythe was such a good actor. No one would guess from the tone of his voice that they were in a gigantic mess.

Mr. Smythe listened to Lynne, agreeing now and then. "Thanks for filling me in. Rest assured I will comfort Chantel and Adam if they need it. But I suspect even if they are upset, there will be distractions. There is so much going on here."

Holly and Owen grinned in spite of themselves.

"Actually, I was going to phone you today," Mr. Smythe continued.

Holly and Owen's eyes widened.

"My friend Mr. Green has invited us to stay for a couple of extra days. Would that be possible? I think the children would enjoy more time here."

Owen recovered first. He grabbed the phone. "Could we, Mum? Please say yes."

They could hear Lynne chuckle. "It's the summer holidays, so why not? Are you finding lots of exciting things to do?"

Owen rolled his eyes. "Loads and loads."

"Then you can stay. I'm glad you are having a good time. Let me know how Chantel and Adam get on and when to expect you back." She rang off.

"Mr. Smythe, that was brilliant! Now we have more time to rescue Adam and the staff," gabbled Owen.

Holly said nothing. She flung her arms around Mr. Smythe and gave him an enormous hug.

The tips of his ears went pink. He patted Holly's back. "I just took advantage of an unexpected opportunity, my dears," he said. "But what about Chantel's mother?"

"Ignore the phone," said Owen.

"We can't do that," protested Holly. "It's Chantel's mum."

"Yes, we can," insisted Owen. "She always makes Chantel cry by going on and on about the divorce."

"Chantel will want to talk to her," insisted Holly.

"We're sunk if she spills the beans," warned Owen.

Right on cue the phone rang again.

Owen and Holly stared at it.

Owen picked up a cushion to muffle the bell.

"Who's calling?" Chantel's voice floated downstairs.

"We think it might be your mum," Holly admitted.

Owen threw the cushion back on its chair.

Chantel half ran, half fell down the stairs. "Answer it!" she yelled.

"Told you," Holly mouthed to her brother. She picked up the receiver. "Hello?...Yes, it's me, Aunt Celia....Yes, Chantel's here, but...but...Adam's out with a friend..." She stared at Chantel, willing her to catch on.

Chantel stared for a moment. She gave a small nod.

Holly handed the receiver to Chantel and patted her shoulder.

"Mom?" said Chantel. She sat on the bottom step of the staircase and hunched over the receiver.

The others retreated into the dining room but openly listened to Chantel's side of the conversation.

"No, Mom, Adam's not here...No, he's not out with a kid...he's with...Mer...Mr. Green, Mr. Smythe's friend, the man whose house we're staying in.

"Er...Yes, we...we're...meeting them later...Yes, of course Mr. Smythe's with us."

There was a long pause at Chantel's end, while her mother talked.

Chantel gave a big sigh. "Mom...It's okay. Me and Adam are getting on fine."

Holly and Owen nudged each other. They had both heard the catch in Chantel's voice.

Owen crossed his fingers and held them up. "Don't cry, Chantel. Don't give anything away," he whispered.

Holly crossed her fingers.

Chantel's voice became shrill, and the stairs creaked as she sat up. "What do you mean, you've solved the problem of us fighting? We're not fighting. It's you and Dad who were fighting...No...NO..." Chantel's voice rose to a shriek. "NO... YOU CAN'T DO THAT...NO WAY." There was a bang as the phone slammed down. Chantel burst into noisy sobs.

Holly and Owen rushed back into the hall. They'd never, ever, heard Chantel shout at her mother.

Holly crouched on the stairs beside her young cousin and hugged her. "It's okay. It's okay."

Chantel shook her head. "It's not. It's awful." She howled into Holly's shoulder.

Holly patted her back but looked baffled. "What's awful, Chantel? What on earth did your mum say?"

Chantel lifted her head. "I hate her, I hate her." She hiccupped. "I thought the worst bit of them getting a divorce would be us not seeing Dad very often." She sobbed and shuddered. "But now they want us to divorce." She buried her head again.

Holly looked baffled. "What do you mean?"

"Spit it out, Chantel," Owen said.

"They...they're sp...splitting us up," hiccupped Chantel. "Mom says I'm to live with her, an...and Adam's going to live with Dad. It's not fair. Just 'cos they're divorcing, why should we be split up? It's not fair. It's just not fair." Chantel's hands covered her face. Tears leaked through her fingers and dripped on the floor. "I wish I was dead. I wish I'd gone through the portal with Adam."

Owen and Holly gazed at each other helplessly over her head.

Chantel pulled herself out of Holly's arms. She dashed her hands over her eyes and ran wildly toward the front door. "I can't take this. I'm going to the Tor. I'm gonna find the portal...and Adam...and I don't care if we never come back."

She pulled the front door open. Mr. Smythe leaped forward to grab her. They stumbled out onto the doorstep.

In a flash of light, Myrddin appeared between them and caught Chantel in his arms.

"Thank goodness!" said Mr. Smythe. "As you can see, we have another crisis."

Chantel wailed. She burrowed deep into Myrddin's cloak.

Myrddin looked at all of them over her head.

"Her mother phoned," said Holly. She briefly recounted the phone call. "It's too much on top of Adam."

Myrddin's face grew sad. He cradled Chantel, wrapping her in his cloak and surrounding her with a feeling of warmth and light.

"Believe in the light, child. Keep it in your heart." To and fro he rocked her, to and fro, whispering in her ear until her weeping stopped, her head dropped and she drifted into a healing sleep.

"You hypnotized her," said Owen in a slightly accusing tone.

Myrddin laid Chantel down on a sofa and covered her with his cloak. "Yes, I hypnotized her. She has suffered enough. Sleep will help heal her bruised heart and give her strength." He dropped his eyes. "She will need strength. We all will."

Owen, Holly and Mr. Smythe exchanged frightened glances.

"We must take counsel," said Myrddin. "Come, let us sit in sunshine, for light keeps fears at bay."

Everyone followed him out to the patio.

"First, you must beware. The Dark Being is within Gaia's orbit. She affects everyone. People will be angry and unpredictable. Weather will be unusual." He looked at the children from under his bushy brows. "She will affect you. You must fight dark feelings."

"We know, we know," muttered Owen. "We have to keep the light in our hearts."

"Indeed," said Myrddin. "Second, we can wait no longer for Equus and Ava."

"Where are they?" Owen said. "They said they'd come!"

"Come they will, but something has detained them."

"We figured out that much," said Owen, "but what?"

Myrddin shook his head. "Peace child. Have faith. The Dark Being watches Gaia. It may be too dangerous for Equus and Ava to approach or to contact me. I am in human form and without my staff. I am helpless."

"Zorianna knows you're here. She'll tell the Dark Being," said Holly.

Myrddin smiled slightly. "Ahh...the first glimmer of hope. My staff and the Mists of Time have dealt with Zorianna. She was prevented from reaching the Dark Being."

"Hurray!" Holly and Owen gave a subdued cheer.

"And the Dark Being thinks I am no threat. She knows I am without my staff. She senses my presence, but knows not where I am hiding."

"But what about Adam?" Holly could stand the suspense no longer. "Where is he? You're saying nothing about him."

She looked at Myrddin's face and saw distress.

Fear clutched at her heart. "He's dead, isn't he?" she said, her voice dull.

Mr. Smythe turned white. His hands trembled.

Myrddin reached out and grasped Holly's and Owen's hands. "No...NO! You must not think that. Adam's not dead. He fell into the darkness."

"W...w...what darkness?" stammered Owen.

Myrddin squeezed their hands tightly as he looked

at Mr. Smythe. "Adam fell and was captured by the Dark Being..."

Holly moaned and closed her eyes.

The color drained from Owen's face. He clenched his fists.

"But there is hope," Myrddin continued.

"Hope! Adam doesn't need hope. He needs us to get him out of there!" burst out Owen. He stood up. "Come on, Myrddin, what are we messing about here for? We have to defeat the Dark Being before she zaps Adam."

Myrddin shook his head. "She will try to use him to learn about Earth Magic and the Tools of Power."

"All the more reason to rescue him first," Holly stood beside Owen.

"Check your warlike feelings," said Myrddin gently.

"I'm not feeling warlike. I'm feeling mad, real MAD," roared Owen. "I've had it with you and the other Wise Ones. What kind of Magical Beings are you, letting Adam be caught? Stop mucking around. We've got to rescue him now! And if you won't, we will."

"Owen's right." Mr. Smythe stood stiffly beside the children. "We *must* rescue Adam."

"Yes, yes, yes," said Myrddin. "Of course we must rescue Adam, but not in anger. Never in anger. That is the most important thing you must learn. Anger feeds the Dark Being, makes her more powerful. It is one of the ways she gains strength." He took several deep, cleansing breaths. "See, she affects even me."

Holly sagged and sat down again. "I get it. It's like the dragon," she said. "That's how we defeated the dragon in the first adventure. Remember Owen? It was feeding on Adam's anger and...and you distracted us all with a stupid song." She began to sing softly, "Nobody likes me, everybody hates me, think I'll go and eat worms..." She trailed off, her eyes anxiously on Owen's.

Several moods flashed over Owen's face. First anger, then derision, then finally his lips quirked in a wry grin and his shoulders relaxed. "Big fat chewy ones, icky, slimy gooey ones," he offered.

"See how they wiggle and squirm," they both warbled. They stopped and gave each other lopsided grins.

"Thanks, Sis," said Owen. He gently punched her arm.

"Feeling better?" asked Myrddin.

Brother and sister nodded.

"Then keep the light in your heart. We will rescue Adam, but we will do it carefully, with help from the Lady."

"NO."

The outburst came from Mr. Smythe.

"No more magic!" He stuffed his hands in his pockets to disguise their shaking.

Myrddin placed a warning hand on Mr. Smythe's shoulder, but spoke softly to the children. "Go inside to Chantel. I sense she is near waking. Then we will plan to help Adam."

He and Mr. Smythe watched them leave.

Adam slept heavily.

While waiting for him to wake, the Dark Being devised

magical spells to penetrate the Mists of Time and Gaia's Earth Magic and reveal Zorianna's whereabouts.

Nothing worked. It was as if the tiny planet below had opened up and swallowed her emissary. There must be more to Gaia than met the eye.

The Dark Being glared down. She and the Shades were poised, ready to destroy, but she wanted Myrddin's staff and Zorianna first. Then it would be such a pleasure to teach the pretty little planet a lesson.

She gazed at the boy sleeping at her feet. What a gift he was! She would use him.

When he woke, she would persuade him to reveal what he'd learned as a Magic Child. Then he would be her slave.

She smiled as a new thought struck her.

If she had a Magic Child, she didn't need Zorianna!

Yes! This boy could go back to Gaia and bring her the staff.

How amusing! A new emissary, a human child who believed she was the Lady. A Magic Child she could use as a hostage.

The Dark Being threw back her head and laughed. The loss of Zorianna no longer mattered.

Still smiling, she returned to watching for a weakness in the Mists of Time, so she could send some Shades to spy on Gaia.

Myrddin's hypnotic whisperings had sent Chantel into a deep sleep. A healing sleep that strengthened her body and her mind. A dark sleep, a telling sleep, where age-old secrets whispered and hidden knowledge stirred. A dreaming sleep, a helpful sleep, where answers hovered.

Chantel slept her way into a safe dark place with solid rock beneath her and at her back. She could hear waves crashing, pounding rhythmically against a cliff below her. As each wave broke, the rock at her back shuddered.

Her body vibrated with the rock, yet she was not afraid. She trusted the rock. She knew it would not give. Not ever!

The waves didn't scare her either. They made a comforting sound, the strong steady pulse of Gaia.

Despite her trust in the safety of the place, Chantel longed for light.

No stars glimmered. No promise of sun lightened the sky. The dark was so thick that without the sound of the sea below, even up and down would be in question. The only certainty in this place was the rock at her back. She leaned against it and wondered why her life was so dark.

Tears flowed.

Meow.

A luminous softness brushed against her arm.

"A white cat! What are you doing here?" Chantel swept the cat into her arms and rubbed her cheek against its fur.

The cat purred and lay still despite the tightness of the child's grip.

Bit by bit, Chantel relaxed.

For a long while, the cat offered warmth and comfort. At last, it lifted its face and rubbed it one last time against Chantel's cheek. With a wriggle the cat slipped from her arms and disappeared.

"Cat, please come back." Chantel's wail cut the night. "I need you." Her eyes searched frantically for the glow of the cat's luminous fur.

The only glimmer was from the few hairs left on one arm of her T-shirt. Chantel stared down at them, three white hairs that gleamed in the dark.

She stretched out her arm and patted the ground beside her. She leaned sideways and touched and stretched farther, beyond the rock. Aah...her hand felt the prickle of grass. She plucked several long stalks and wove them blindly together into a clumsy ball. One by one, she lifted the three hairs off her sleeve and inserted them into the woven ball.

The hairs glowed.

Chantel scrambled to her feet. Her heart flooded with hope and her body flooded with renewed energy. She could be strong like the rock. She could fight darkness.

She had made a lantern. She had made light!

The more she rejoiced, the stronger the light became.

Holding the small lantern high, she looked around. She was at the top of a cliff. Waves crashed magnificently below. The dim light reflected on foaming white crests that looked like the tossing manes of horses charging toward the shore to surround and protect her.

Remembering Equus, Chantel smiled. *I am always here*, he had said when she first met him. Maybe he was.

<hr />

"Chantel. Chantel...Wake up." A voice echoed through the darkness. Someone was calling her. A voice she knew. She must go back.

Chantel lifted the homemade lantern once again and made her way around the rock, away from the cliff edge, through the blackness. She moved with assurance, stepping to the beat of the waves, knowing she was not alone. She was not helpless. Equus would always be there in her heart, and her own actions could create light. She emerged from her dark sleep into the sunlight.

The three cousins held a hurried meeting sitting on Chantel's sofa.

Chantel's new-found confidence was shaken when she heard of Adam's capture, but she held her emotions in check.

"We're going to rescue Adam and wake the Lady," said Holly, holding Chantel's hand in a firm grip.

"We have to lose Mr. Smythe," said Owen. "He'll try to stop us. He's terrified."

"Let's find him a job to do," said Holly. "Remember how helpful he was when we were looking for the Red Mare? He needs something to keep him busy while we do magic." She looked at the others. "You realize that's what we have to do, don't you? We have to start doing more and more Earth Magic on our own. And we should split up to do it so there's three times more Earth Magic working and growing."

Chantel's eyes were enormous. "I get to do magic on my own?"

"Especially you," said Holly. "You were the first Magic Child. You were the first to hear Equus."

She stood up and stretched. "It's odd. I'm terrified for

Adam, and I know things are getting worse, but I have this feeling deep inside my heart that something's changed and it's going to work out."

Chantel leapt up and threw her arms around her cousin's waist. "I love you, Holly Berry." She reached out and grasped Owen's hand. "You too."

Owen looked embarrassed, but he didn't snatch his hand away. He returned a big squeeze.

"Holly's right," continued Chantel. "Let's stir up enough magic to beat the Dark Being and get Adam back."

As Holly and Owen left the patio to wake Chantel, Myrddin touched Mr. Smythe's arm again. "We need a private talk, my friend."

"We certainly do," agreed Mr. Smythe grimly.

They stepped down into the garden out of earshot of the children.

Mr. Smythe looked bitterly at Myrddin. "You and your magic," he said.

Myrddin did not meet his eyes.

"This is hell. You must get Adam back without delay. He must be terrified. I am." Mr. Smythe glared at Myrddin. "I've been entrusted with the children. And I trusted you. How can I explain Adam's disappearance to his parents, and his aunt and uncle?" Mr. Smythe shook his finger. "Find Adam now. Only you can do it. And you must not put the other children in danger. I'm taking them home. You should never have involved children."

"We never intended to involve children," said Myrddin.

"They were the only humans who heard our messages. In your world, magic is almost gone. No adults hear us or believe in us. Even you have trouble believing what is happening."

Mr. Smythe dropped his eyes.

"The children offered assistance of their own free will," continued Myrddin. "It was their offer combined with their belief in the Old Magic and their innocence of the nature of darkness that enabled them to outwit the Dark Being and her supporters."

"Then they have played their part. Now it is too dangerous to continue," Mr. Smythe said. His voice was stern. "The children could have been killed several times over. They were lucky. But not lucky enough. This time, Adam failed. He is lost, and Zorianna has your staff. It is over."

Myrddin shook his head and smiled. "No, my friend. Adam did not fail. Not only was he able to unlock the Earth Magic that bound the staff within the Tor, but by hanging onto Zorianna's cloak he slowed her down. He gave Old Magic time to respond. The Mists of Time have been inactive for years. Now they are alive again, protecting Earth. They helped prevent Zorianna's escape.

"The sorcerer Manannan has confined Zorianna and she is unable to return to the Dark Being." Myrddin clasped Mr. Smythe's hands. "Adam gave us a victory, my friend. Zorianna and my staff are held in a place of safety, imprisoned by Earth Magic." He smiled. "We *will* rescue Adam. Then the Magic Children have another chance to succeed."

"I'm taking them home," repeated Mr. Smythe.

"My dear Smythe, the Dark Being and her Shades are upon us. Gaia is on the verge of total annihilation. Don't you realize what is happening? Wars are erupting in all parts of the world. No earthly superpower with armies and bombs can end these conflicts. They are fuelled by the Dark Being's presence. However..." Myrddin peered under his bushy eyebrows at his friend. "However...Holly, Owen, and Chantel have the power to save both Adam and Gaia. Will you prevent them from doing that?"

Mr. Smythe pulled his hands from Myrddin's grasp. "The children are in my care," he muttered. "I must protect them. I cannot allow them to face more danger."

"Yes, we must protect them. They are Adam's and Gaia's only hope," repeated Myrddin.

The two old men stared at each other.

"We know we are Adam's and Gaia's only hope," said a quiet voice. "We will carry on."

Myrddin and Mr. Smythe swung around.

Holly stood above them, looking down over the edge of the patio. Owen and Chantel stood on her either side. All three children seemed to have grown in stature.

"We know we are the only ones who can do Earth Magic," said Holly gravely. "And you both know we cannot go home without Adam. We will continue to help you, Myrddin." She smiled at Mr. Smythe. "Thank you for trying to protect us, Mr. Smythe. But you must understand. There is no one else."

"Yup. We have to get Adam back, and if we don't help Gaia, we're all goners anyway," said Owen. His bluntness made Mr. Smythe cringe.

"The Wise Ones' light will help and protect us," said Chantel. Conviction rang though her words, and her eyes sparked with fervor.

"You must both help us, for we have no other choice. Let's conquer the Dark Being. Then we can all go home." Owen put his arm around Chantel and gave her a squeeze. "And we'll think of a way to fix your mom," he whispered.

"Thank you, Magic Children." Myrddin bowed regally to them.

The three children bowed awkwardly back.

Mr. Smythe threw up his hands.

"There is no time to waste," said Myrddin, as everyone gathered in the dining room. "We must re-enter the portal on Glastonbury Tor. The Mists have deposited Zorianna within the magic realm of Mann, the most mysterious part of Gaia, an island known to you humans as The Isle of Man. Her arrival there was no accident, for on that island the fourth Wise One sleeps. We will travel there."

Holly gasped. "To the Lady!"

"Yes, Holly. We will go to Mann, retrieve my staff from Zorianna and wake the Lady. She will have the power to save Adam."

Holly gave a little sigh of satisfaction. "So it *is* my turn to help."

"This magical island," interrupted Mr. Smythe. "Can it only be reached through the portal?" He struggled for the right words. "I mean...is it the magic realm you go to...or the real island? I ask because I know the Isle of Man."

Myrddin nodded. "It is both. Isle of Man is an earthly place. But like the Tor, it exists in magic realms at the same time. People live there, but most are unaware of the depths of its magic."

"So why go through the portal?" said Mr. Smythe. "Why not travel as normal people?"

"Time," replied Myrddin. "Magic is fast. We must be there and back in time for you to take the children home."

Mr. Smythe smiled. "For once I am ahead of you, Myrddin. While you were in the Mists of Time, I asked Holly and Owen's mother if we could stay a couple of extra days...to give you time to find Adam."

Myrddin's face lit up. "Despite all your misgivings, you are still my friend. Thank you for your support."

"Not so fast. Not so fast, Myrddin," Mr. Smythe said. "You want my involvement? You have it. The children and I will come with you..." He held up his hand to quell the response. "But listen to my terms. Magic must be kept to the minimum. No more dashing through dangerous portals. I'll take you. Have you forgotten I'm a pilot? I'll hire a plane. We'll fly."

The childrens eyes sparkled.

"That's going to keep him busy for a while," whispered Holly. "Earth Magic, here we come."

CHAPTER THREE

A BROKEN THREAD

Holly shoved the last items into her backpack ready for the trip to Isle of Man, then crept out to the garden and sat behind a rose bush. She timed it for when she could hear Owen and Chantel making plans with Myrddin, and the drone of Mr. Smythe's voice as he phoned about the plane.

It was time to do what she had urged Owen and Chantel to do, time to try working magic for herself. If the Lady wasn't contacting her, she would try to contact the Lady.

Holly organized several objects in front of her, a small glass of water, a tea light and some matches. She lit the tea light, picked a fragrant rose from the bush beside her and held it while she thought. She needed to speak directly to the Lady, the same way Arto had during their adventure in the heart of the Tor. If she did it right, maybe the Lady would speak back.

She took a deep breath.

"Dear Lady, please hear me. I think something is wrong because we need you, and you're not awake.

"I kneel on the earth with the elements of fire and water." She picked up the rose and wafted it gently. "I fill the air with perfume for you. Please wake up.

"If you cannot wake, please send me a dream. Show me how to help you."

Holly crossed her legs and laid her hands on her knees, palms up in the classic yoga position, and closed her eyes.

"I'm listening, Lady...Please talk to me."

A light breeze carried the scent of roses all around her. She breathed deeply. She could also smell wet earth and the sweet honey aroma of heather, mixed with a tang of salt. The breeze must be blowing inland from the coast. The city sounds of traffic died away, and the air filled with the cry of gulls...

Holly's eyes snapped open. The breeze had become a chilly wind from the sea. Myrddin's garden was gone. She was ankle deep in prickly heather at the base of a tall round tower rising from the center of a rocky islet. Gulls wheeled above, and she could hear waves breaking close by.

Holly crept along the tower's base, hugging its walls and peering carefully around their curve in case someone—or something—dangerous was hidden on the other side. The tower was very odd. It seemed to have no entrance.

A raven croaked.

AARCK.

Holly looked up.

The raven was perched on the sill of a narrow slit, one of several small windows at the top of the tower.

Windows were to give light, so there must be a room up there. And there was the door, but it was useless. It opened high above her head, halfway up the side of the tower. No steps led to it.

Holly shook her head. It was clear she wasn't on this windy wet islet to go inside the tower.

The islet was tiny. From the base of the tower she could see the shoreline. The islet lay not far from land, between a river estuary and a wide sandy bay.

The tide was out, and for the moment an exposed sandbank joined the islet to a headland. Across the sandbank was a trail of footprints.

Holly crept farther around the tower and froze.

On the rock-strewn slope below her stood the group of people who must have made the footprints. Some were young, some old. All seemed distressed. They'd gathered around a depression in the ground.

Not sure if she was in a trance, dreaming, or somehow really there, Holly didn't approach in case she could be seen. She huddled by the tower and watched.

The women pulled woolen shawls over their heads and shoulders, and began to keen in high thin voices. The children, hanging onto their mother's skirts, covered their ears and buried their heads in the heavy fabric.

The men, most dressed in woolen tunics with

sheepskins around their shoulders, stood by, still and silent.

No one seemed aware of Holly, and she was too far away to see what they were looking at.

Step by careful step, Holly inched her way down the uneven slope until she could peep between two young people. She stiffened and covered her mouth to silence a gasp.

She was witnessing a burial.

A dead woman, swathed in a hooded cloak of brown woven wool, lay in a shallow grave lined with rock slabs. Her face was uncovered.

Holly's eyes slid away. She had never seen a dead body before.

No. She must look. This was why she was here. Taking a deep breath to steel herself, Holly made herself watch.

The body wasn't really scary. The woman looked as though she was sleeping, only more still. In fact she was beautiful, not like a film star, but with an ageless beauty, seeming neither young nor old. Her skin was as white and waxen as a magnolia blossom.

"Ah, Breesha, Breesha, I miss thy friendship and wise counsel." A woman with two small children stepped forward and scattered a handful of wild flowers and fragrant herbs over the body.

Holly smelled wild garlic, mint, rosemary and roses.

"May these herbs protect thee and ease thy journey into the mist, as thy medicines and spells eased our lives."

A second woman came forward. She held out a small cloth bag. "Many's the time thou baked our bread, Breesha.

I thank thee and give thee flour for thy journey." She knelt and tucked the bag into the folds of the cloak.

"And I give thee seeds thou loved in a bag of thy garden's soil. Use them in next spring's planting in thy new world beyond the mist." A third woman dropped a tiny leather bag beside the body.

"I give thee a jug of the sacred water from Spooyt Vane to refresh you," said a soft voice, as a young woman, barely out of her teens, placed a sealed water pot in the crook of Breesha's arm.

One by one, other members of the group stepped forward with gifts. Needles, shears, a workbox, a knife, a pestle and mortar, and a flint and some feathers were placed in the grave.

Finally everyone returned to the circle and waited.

Holly's eyes prickled with tears. The woman was someone who was loved and respected. She must also have used magic, for elements of earth, air, fire and water had been given to her.

A tall husky man took his place at the head of Breesha's grave. He was the odd one out. Instead of being short and stocky with dark hair and eyes, this man's red hair flamed and he towered over everyone. He held a long metal rod in his hand.

"We named you Breesha, a name from Mann," he said, "for you traveled nameless from the Mists of Time to our settlement. You brought wisdom and peace. You kept my hearth fire, became my helpmate and mother of my children. You showed us all how people from two lands could live together in peace."

The people around the grave nodded.

Holly realized the man was a different race from the other adults. She stared around the group. It was clear some of the children were a mix of both races. While most were short and dark haired, several sported the red hair or tall stature of the man.

The red-haired man looked down sadly.

"Now your spirit travels back into the Mists from whence you came, Breesha. We wish you well and give you everything needed to comfort your journey, and earth, air, fire and water to protect you.

"When you came to Mann, great magic came with you. So we bury you in a magic place surrounded by water, as you requested. We give you back the metal staff you wielded, the sign of a sorceress." The man knelt, parted the cloak and tucked the rod beside the woman's body.

"Wait," came a cry. "Where is Breesha's necklace?"

The woman who had scattered herbs and flowers over the body pointed to where the cloak had fallen open at the neck, exposing Breesha's chest.

A buzz of consternation ran around the group.

The man leapt to his feet and turned to glare at a woman on the opposite side of the grave. "Mona, you washed and dressed Breesha's body."

The woman named Mona held her own dark cloak tightly clasped to her chin. Her eyes met his defiantly.

A raven broke the silence.

AARCK. AARCK.

The cry galvanized the man to action.

He strode over and roughly twisted the woolen fabric

from Mona's fingers. He ripped her tunic at the neck and thrust her forward so all could see.

A fabulous necklace of polished stones and glass spilled out and swung down against her upper body. Every bead was a different color and size. Some were colored glass, some were polished stones. Holly glimpsed beads of gold, of red, malachite, silver, and turquoise, and a large amber disk hanging from the center.

Mona's fingers closed desperately over the necklace. She bunched the beads up into her palms and clutched them against her chest. "Bury not the beads with Breesha. They carry too much magic. The necklace should pass to me. I carry the spell bundle and have the healing skills. I am the next sorceress. Breesha chose me." Her voice rose to a shriek.

The man's eyes flashed, and the woman cowered. She froze as he stepped forward, pried apart her fingers and lifted the necklace over her head.

Mona quivered, though whether with rage or fright Holly couldn't tell.

The man returned to the body. He knelt, gently lifted Breesha's head and slipped the necklace around her neck.

"Thou dost right, Sigurd. The necklace came with Breesha. It never left her neck in life. She must keep it in death," said a voice from the crowd.

"Thou dost not understand," cried Mona. She ran forward and grabbed Sigurd's arm. "Stay thy hand." She glared around at the group. "The necklace has a magic more powerful than anything we own. Think before thou forfeit it so easily. 'Twas Breesha's magic that saved us from deadly illness and starvation."

"Breesha's magic was her own. Some she chose to share with you, Mona. She gave you her spell bundle, and you learned many of her skills. Be content and do not desecrate her memory," said the red-haired man harshly. "The necklace came from the mist with Breesha. Breesha requested it accompany her return." He pushed Mona away.

She stumbled, lost her balance and sprawled across the body. Her hand caught in the loop of the necklace.

The necklace snapped.

Beads scattered.

Everyone gasped. A terrible silence fell.

Mona raised herself up on her arms and looked down in horror at Breesha's body.

Hands grabbed her, pulling back on her shoulders, dragging her from the grave.

Mona shook herself free, adjusted her cloak and stared defiantly at the mourners. "That was not my doing."

All dropped their eyes.

"Thou wilt regret this," she spat and ran swiftly down the narrow track, between the rocks and heather, her cloak ends flapping like black wings.

For a moment, no one moved.

"The beads must be replaced," said a soft voice. A young girl knelt reverently by Breesha's body. She began picking up the scattered gems. "Help me remember the order and place them right."

The women moved forward, and one by one the beads were gathered and placed together, silver against malachite, red glass again against turquoise, in the order all remembered.

The young girl wedged them, so each bead touched its neighbor, propped with delicate folds of the cloak. Finally she laid the large disk of amber over Breesha's heart.

"It is done," said the girl.

Sigurd shook out a square of fine white linen and covered Breesha's face.

He made a gesture of finality and stood back.

Several men lifted three flat slabs of sandstone and sealed the tomb.

Sigurd held up a small plank of wood. "I am charged to fill Breesha's last request. The secret name of a sorceress holds great magic. To know it brings power. None of us knew Breesha's secret name. Before she passed, the Mists of Time parted and showed Breesha a vision, a child of the future in need of her secret name." Sigurd held up a board covered with scratched lines.

"Breesha recorded her name of power so the future child can read it. Behold it, concealed within the magic runes." He laid the board on top of the stone slabs.

The mourners looked at it uncomprehendingly.

Sigurd pick up a white quartz rock. "Let us complete

Breesha's cairn." He placed his rock on top of the board.

The people gathered loose boulders of the gleaming quartz scattered around the islet. The men chose large ones and the women and children picked the smaller ones. They were mounded around and on top of Breesha's grave, covering the slabs, the board and the sides of the tomb in a glowing white pile. The people toiled in silence.

By now the light was fading and the tide rising. With it came threads of sea mist that drifted between the mourners.

Sigurd signaled everyone to stop. "It is done. We must take our leave." He placed a hand on one of the rocks. "Everything you asked is done, Breesha. I call upon the raven to guide you and the Black Dog to protect you as you travel through the Mists of Time."

AARCK, called the raven.

A distant howl echoed. The mist stirred.

Holly and all the mourners shivered. The men drew their sheepskins more tightly around their shoulders, and the women held their children close.

Each mourner stepped forward, touched the white cairn and left without looking back. They ran across the remains of the sandbank and disappeared into the gathering gloom.

Sigurd lingered. He bent and whispered to the cairn in a strange tongue, laid a hand on the stones and strode away.

Holly was alone. She stepped forward and placed her own hand on one of the white rocks. Was this a dream? Would she feel it?

The quartz was hard and cold.

Holly shivered. "Breesha, are you the Lady?" she whispered. "Is that why I am at your funeral? Am I the child from the future? Am I supposed to understand the scratches on the wood?" She shrugged, "I don't."

No voice spoke to her. No vision came. She had no clue as to what she should do next.

Holly felt helpless and alone. She was cold and stiff from standing still. The mist closing in was creepy. She peered down the rapidly disappearing track, wondering if she should follow everyone.

"I can't stay here," she mused out loud. "The tide will cut me off." She stepped onto the track.

Her toe kicked a small stone. It rolled before her: black, shiny and perfectly round.

Holly picked it up. It was a bead, a polished jet bead.

Holly swung back and looked with dawning horror at the rocky cairn that rose over the grave. "They missed a bead!" she cried. She ran to the cairn and began to tear the rock pile apart. "Breesha, one of your magic beads was forgotten." Holly uncovered the edge of one sandstone slab. She pushed against it. It was immovable. "Come on, you pig," she grunted as she thrust using all her weight. "I just need a crack to drop the bead in. Come ON. Move, you pig! Move, move, MOVE!"

It was no good. The slab was too heavy.

"What should I do?" Holly held her clasped hand up to the sky. "Breesha, tell me what to do?"

Tatters of mist blew around her.

"I can't take the bead back with me," Holly yelled. "Been there, done that. I took the Glastonbury cup in the last adventure, and it caused me all kinds of problems."

The wind blew harder. Ice-cold rain began to fall.

Holly turned to the grave again. She pounded on the slab. "Breesha, listen to me," she shouted. "I've found your bead, so I'll put it as close to you as I can." Holly knelt beside the grave and scrabbled with her fingers and a sharp rock. She scraped down into the hard ground beside two upright slabs that lined the grave. She found a crack, a joint, and followed it down into the earth, scraping away what dirt she could, looking for a small gap that would go through to the tomb. It was no use, the rock liners butted too closely together.

Distressed, Holly stamped back the dirt, then replaced the stones she had removed from the cairn.

"Okay...I get it, Breesha...I have to take the bead." Holly reluctantly stuffed it deep in the pocket of her jeans.

She was cold and wet and exhausted. Her fingers were numb, and blood oozed from several scratches.

Holly sucked her knuckles and blew into cupped hands to warm them. She hunkered down for shelter between two large clumps of heather. To her surprise, the heather was thick enough to offer real protection. It deflected both wind and rain. The closer she huddled to the ground, the more shelter she gained. She stretched out on her stomach and lay down among the roots, her head cushioned on her arms, listening to the rustling of wind and the patter of rain.

A stone clinked.

Holly's heart leaped. She peered up through the vegetation.

A black figure loomed beside the cairn.

It was Mona.

Holly flattened herself into the ground, holding her breath, afraid that this woman with a knowledge of magic would see her.

But Mona saw nothing but the cairn. She rolled rock after rock to the ground. With a cry of triumph, she pulled out the oak board. "SO...the whispers I overheard were true," she hissed. She held the board up to the fading light and traced each line with her fingers. She growled with frustration. "What magic is this? These scratches are symbols I know not!" Mona stared at the board again. "I swear I will learn thy name of power, Breesha, or pass the board to another who can."

A dog howled.

Mona flung the rocks back, tucked the board under her cloak and fled silently into the mist.

Holly heard her splashing through the incoming tide.

AARCK, AARCK, AARCK, called a raven.

Holly stiffly rose from her hollow in the heather. She tried to see through the mist. "Raven, are you trying to tell me something?" she asked.

She heard only the creaking of wings as the bird flew away.

Now Holly was really alone. She was scared.

The mist swept around and enclosed her in a great gray blanket. She could see nothing, hear nothing, feel nothing...

⬚⬚⬚⬚⬚

"Holly! Holly...where are you?" Chantel's voice came from the other side of the rose bush. "There you are." She appeared in front of Holly, gasping for breath. "We couldn't find you," she said. "Mr. Smythe's hired a floatplane, so we have to drive to the river at Bristol. Come and load your stuff." She stopped and glanced down at the water glass and tea light. "Oh...you've done some magic?"

Holly stretched her stiff limbs and gave an embarrassed grin. Her heart was thumping; she was cold and confused. "Sort of...The Lady still hasn't talked to me, so I was trying to contact her...," she trailed off.

"Did it work? Have you met her?"

Holly gathered together the glass, the tea light and matches and clambered to her feet. She rubbed her head. "I'm not sure. It was strange. Let's find Owen and I'll fill you both in."

Mr. Smythe's Land Rover was quickly loaded, and they were off, swiftly moving down the motorway toward Bristol and the Avon River estuary. The three children huddled in the backseat, heads together. Myrddin sat stiffly in the front passenger seat, bracing himself with one hand on the dashboard. He hated all forms of human-designed transportation.

"I tried some magic," hissed Owen, one eye on Mr. Smythe in case he overheard. "I tried to talk to Ava, and I went into a kind of trance. Nothing really happened. It was just weird. Everything whirled around me, and I was terrified. It was as though I was in whirlpool or the middle of a hurricane. Then I saw a white feather floating toward me. I thought it was real and from Ava. I tried to grab it. Then I was back in the bedroom and I'd grabbed my toothbrush off the dresser."

Chantel giggled. "You're so weird."

Holly rolled her eyes. "Wait till you hear what happened in my vision, toothbrush man..." She pulled out the black bead.

Chantel and Owen groaned.

"Idiot. Didn't you get into enough trouble last time you brought something back from dream-magic?" hissed Owen.

Holly shrugged. "I didn't have a choice, here's what happened..."

CHAPTER FOUR

Island Magic

In the Kingdom of Mann, Manannan braced himself as Zorianna fell into his portal. Ripping through the webbed magic, she plunged into the secret caverns below the castle on Pheric's Isle.

Manannan repaired the web and waited.

He didn't have to wait long.

A rumbling growl followed by the baying of a great dog echoed throughout the castle ruins.

The Moddy Dhoo had begun to prowl.

Manannan sighed.

The Black Dog was an ancient, unpredictable magic, far older than himself. It protected Old Magic and could not be directed. Its current charge was the Sleeper. As he had feared, Zorianna was a threat to her.

FLASH!

Manannan shape-changed into his most fearsome form, one not seen on Mann for hundreds of years, one he used to conceal his identity from enemies while terrifying them. He became three armored legs, joined at the thigh, spinning within a great wheel of fire.

The wheel of fire rolled down the slopes of Barrule, across the water and into the castle's secret passages.

※※※※

The Moddy Dhoo raised its black head and sniffed the darkness, seeking the scent of the intruder. It left its lair beneath the castle's ruined gatehouse and bound into the secret passages, pausing and sniffing eagerly at each twist and turn. It had not hunted prey for hundreds of years.

The Black Dog could be sensed but not seen. Its fur blended with the night for it was darker than darkness. The Moddy Dhoo was more feared than the dark. The giant dog *was* darkness.

※※※※

Zorianna's precipitous entrance through the magic portal alerted a second ancient entity.

A white cat with no tail prowled the secret passages, avoiding the path of the Moddy Dhoo.

White as moonlight and silent as light, the cat was a pale gleam in the dark. She was a guide between the worlds and, unlike the Moddy Dhoo, offered light.

The darkness behind the cat thickened and growled.

The white cat spat and arched high, leaping out of the way.

The passage cleared, the Moddy Dhoo passed on, sniffing the air.

The cat followed, keeping to the high dark ledge.

A sliver of silver drifted down.

One hair. A thread of light in the dark.

Dark and Light. Light and Dark.

At this moment on Gaia, the darkness was very dark indeed.

***

It was a strange day on the Isle of Man.

Instead of blue skies and warm August sunshine, a creeping gray fog hung in the air, obscuring everything. In the town of Peel, the fog was so thick no one could see across the narrow winding streets. It was an eerie fog, filled with the sound of wings from the passage of restless gulls.

The commotion and the fog seemed to center around tiny Pheric's Isle across the bay, where the birds on the ruined walls of ancient Peel Castle could be heard screaming defiance at the top of their voices.

People leaving their homes for work, cussed at the fog and wafted impatient hands at the mist veils, trying to spot the cause of the gulls' unrest.

Nothing could be seen. Thick threads of sea mist drifted to and fro, concealing all but the haziest outline of the castle.

The incessant screams of the gulls echoed around the town.

Old Mr. Cubbon walked stiffly out to the inner harbor and stared across the tidal flats of the River Nebb.

"Hush, you!" he shouted at the birds. "Hush yer screamin' and give us the skeet." He cupped his ear and listened.

The screaming died down a little.

AARCK.

A ruffled-looking raven soared through the fog and landed beside the old man.

Mr. Cubbon threw it a piece of toast. "There yer are, Blacky. Come for yer treat as usual. Go on then. Give us the skeet. I'm listenin'."

The raven picked at the toast. Then, turning its head to one side, it looked piercingly at Mr. Cubbon and uttered a series of cries.

The old man cupped his hand over his ear and listened intently.

His gossip shared, Blacky spread his wings and soared back to Pheric's Isle, taking the remaining toast with him.

Mr. Cubbon followed Blacky's flight until the bird was swallowed by the mist. His face was grave. He gave a sudden shudder. "Sommat's walkin' over my grave," he muttered. "Aye, an' I know what. Yon Moddy Dhoo's prowlin'. Old Magic's awake."

In the Place Beyond Morning, shadows fled as Ava and Equus combined their power to raise the shattered Gates of Sunrise at last. Once more, pure light poured through. It washed over and awakened the land.

"Now it is safe to leave and return to the children," panted Ava.

Equus looked with pride at their home, from the sun sparkling again on the tips of the Crystal Mountains, to the brilliant sheen of the Silver Citadel.

The sunlight poured in, creating a land of promise. Birds sang in a deafening chorus. Spring flowers budded. Fields and trees greened, and water tumbled through long-dry streambeds.

"Never again will we allow the Dark Being to smash these gates and deprive the universe of light and hope," said Equus.

Equus and Ava stood together beneath the Gates of Sunrise and bowed in the direction of Gaia. "Thank you, Magic Children, for the return of the talisman and circlet."

They both staggered under a sudden blast of mindspeak.

"The children! The children are in more trouble," said Ava. She listened, her face grave. "This is old mindspeak. It couldn't reach us until we raised the gates and the light streamed through."

"We must return at once to Gaia," said Equus. "Dare we risk sending a message?"

Ava shook her head. "Even travel is risky. The Dark One's emissaries are everywhere."

Dimming their own light, Equus galloped and Ava soared in his wake, first along sunbeams then among moonbeams, concealing themselves on their journey across the universe, Equus suddenly dug in his hooves and slid to a halt. Ava circled and landed on his back.

All was not well around the planet they called Gaia and

the children called Earth. There was a strange thickening in the Mists of Time.

The great horse and hawk peered upward through the brightness, surveying the galaxy for clues.

Ava gasped and Equus stiffened.

The black cloud had cleared, and something dark and terrible pulsed and spun in the middle of the Milky Way.

"The Dark Being has called her Shades together. Look how they circle around her, causing a whirling black hole." Equus shuddered. "That vortex could swallow us all. Our light may not be strong enough."

Ava stared in horror, scarcely believing what she saw. She steadied herself and began to speak. "I have heard tell of an ancient way to help dissipate a vortex. When Shades take this form, there is a way to let in a beam of light." She shivered. "The way is risky, but if I succeed, the light will create a tiny chink in the dark. A crack straight into the Dark Being's heart."

"How can we let in light?" asked Equus.

"By using the Dark Being's own power," replied Ava. "The vortex draws all toward her. It is her strength, but also her weakness." She took a deep breath. "Equus, we must use the vortex. It may be our only chance to weaken her."

Without waiting for Equus to reply, Ava shape-shifted into a tiny hawk. Using her beak, she plucked a small white feather from her breast. She flew onto her companion's back and swiftly wound a fine silver hair from Equus' mane around the feather's shaft and gave a sharp tug.

His skin twitched.

"Ava, this is too dangerous. What about the children?"

"Hush, Equus. The Dark Being is distracted. There couldn't be a better time. For the sake of Gaia and the universe, the children must wait."

Ava touched Equus with her wing and took off, flying swiftly, circling toward the vortex.

Equus watched as Ava became a speck against the brightness of the Milky Way. Was she small enough to escape detection? Was she strong enough to escape the pull of the vortex?

Deep in the dungeons of Peel Castle, Zorianna slumped against a cold damp wall. The fight with Myrddin's staff had drained her. She was spent and sick of Earth Magic. It held too many nasty surprises. The stars only knew where it had deposited her this time.

Zorianna rubbed her head to try to clear it. She longed to rest but dared not. Tipping her head back against the wall, she tried to make sense of her situation.

Earth Magic had captured her. She was somewhere on Gaia, enclosed within the earth and surrounded by water—she loathed the distant hiss of waves. Would they never stop rising and falling?

In the background floated the muffled cries of birds. The agents of air kept watch.

Zorianna shuddered. The barriers of earth, air and water made this the most powerful place she had discovered on the humans' planet. She was thankful that there was no magical fire. Maybe that was a weakness she could explore...

Before she could complete the thought, a great heat poured down the passages toward her.

She jumped to her feet and reached for Myrddin's staff. She knew she couldn't trust it, but she had no magic left. The staff was her only option.

The approaching Earth Magic was almost upon her. The muscles in Zorianna's arms trembled as she heaved and tugged to raise Myrddin's stubborn staff.

"Give me light!" she ordered as she finally managed to pull the weighty object upright. "Shield me with light!"

The crystal at the top of the staff glowed for a moment, no more.

"I command you, staff!" screamed Zorianna. "I wield you, and danger approaches. You are required to protect me. Shield me with light!"

A flare spurted from the crystal on top of the staff.

Zorianna's eyes snapped shut against its sudden brilliance.

She did not see the light split into four thin strands that curled back and forth, winding up, down and around her body, arms and legs.

The crystal dimmed.

Zorianna opened her eyes.

She looked down at the glowing bonds. Their light formed a shield around her, but also bound her wrists and feet. With a howl of anger, she hurled the staff as far as her restricted arms would allow.

The staff thudded to the floor and rolled into a dark corner out of her sight.

A second, more fearsome light blazed. A wheel of

fire whirled down the passage and came to a halt before her.

Zorianna closed her eyes and gathered together her remaining courage. This place was a nightmare. Now she was confronted by fire, the element that completed the circle of Earth Magic.

She leaned against the wall for support and tried to stop her bound body from shrinking from the heat.

"YOU WISHED FOR LIGHT. I BRING IT," roared a voice from within the fire. Armored legs inside the flames revolved almost faster than she could see, threatening to mow her down. "WHO ARE YOU THAT TUMBLES UNINVITED THROUGH THE MISTS AND RENTS MY SECRET PORTAL?"

Zorianna drew herself up as straight as her bonds allowed. Her eyes flashed. "I am Zorianna, emissary of the Dark Being. Who are you?"

Her question was ignored.

"WHY HAS THE STAFF OF THE MYRDDIN BOUND YOU? WHY DID I SENSE FEAR AND TURMOIL WITH YOUR APPROACH?"

"The fear was not from me," said Zorianna. "It came from the puny human child who hung onto my cloak. He has gone and is of no consequence."

"NO CONSEQUENCE?" roared the voice. "YOU ARE MISTAKEN. HUMANS ARE ALWAYS OF CONSEQUENCE. HUMANS HOLD THE WELLBEING OF THE UNIVERSE WITHIN THEIR EARTH MAGIC."

Zorianna laughed harshly. "You jest. The Dark Being holds the fate of the universe."

The wheel of fire revolved faster, and its flames crackled as it considered Zorianna's answer.

"SO...YOU DO NOT UNDERSTAND...YOU THINK YOU HAVE POWER BECAUSE YOU REPRESENT SHE WHO WOULD BRING DARKNESS TO GAIA? BE AWARE THAT DARKNESS RESIDES HERE ALREADY."

As the voice of fire spoke, Zorianna saw the darkness behind it thicken.

She gave a snort. "I have experience of your Earth Magic. It is weak and simple. The Dark Being has no equal and is all powerful. When she comes, Gaia will bow to her command or be destroyed. Even you."

"NEITHER YOU NOR SHE WILL BE ALLOWED TO FIND THE POWER SHE SEEKS. WHAT WILL HAPPEN WHEN YOU FAIL?" The flames glowed.

Zorianna realized she was turning her head from side to side to escape the heat that frizzled her hair and seared her skin.

Flickers of fear threatened to weaken her, but she was also intrigued at what was being said. She closed her eyes against the brightness, held her head high and jutted her chin once more. "*Allowed* is an interesting word. Nothing can stop the Dark Being from finding the power she seeks. I cannot and will not fail."

"AHH! YOU DO NOT YET UNDERSTAND THE LINK BETWEEN THE LIGHT AND THE DARK. YOU WILL LEARN, AND I HAVE LEARNED ENOUGH. *LHIAT MYR HOILOO*—TO THEE AS THOU DESERVEST."

Abruptly the wheel left.

Zorianna's knees trembled. She slid down the wall onto the floor with a sigh of relief. She had no idea what curse or spell had been flung at her, but she had not been engaged in a battle. She could rest, regain some strength, and figure out the tiresome Earth Magic that confined her. She placed her bound arms on her knees and rested her head against them.

The light from Zorianna's bonds continued to glow. It reflected in two sets of watching eyes.

The Moddy Dhoo settled before her on the floor.

A safe distance away, the cat sat up.

Both waited in silence.

It would be some time before Zorianna roused and noticed them.

Mr. Smythe piloted the small floatplane containing the three children and Myrddin across Wales and out over the Irish Sea toward the Isle of Man.

It was a golden day for flying, and Mr. Smythe was in his element. Despite his worry about Adam, he felt the years drop from him as he handled the controls of the six-seater Beaver. He was in charge of something at last, and no magic was involved. He whistled snatches of old army marching songs.

The children relaxed. They all enjoyed flying, and the novelty of taking off in a floatplane from the Avon Estuary and seeing the countryside from the air kept them glued to the windows for the first part of the flight.

Leaving the coast and droning over the Irish Sea was

less interesting. Owen and Chantel slept, catching up after their adventurous night on the Tor helping Adam find Myrddin's staff.

Holly was too worried to sleep. She gazed blankly out of the plane window, mulling over Adam's fate, her vision of Breesha and the bead. She must get Myrddin on his own to ask his advice.

She lifted her head to look at him.

He sat at the front, beside Mr. Smythe, holding tight to the plane as if his clenched fists had the power to keep it in the air. He had been silent for the whole flight, she realized. He was worried too and not just about the flying.

Holly sighed. Mr. Smythe was so terrified that some awful magic would happen that he wouldn't let Myrddin out of his sight. He had made sure the children had no chance to talk to him.

Myrddin must know who Breesha was. Surely she couldn't be the Lady. Other than the fabulous necklace, she wasn't grand or magical looking like the other Wise Ones. And she was dead! A Wise One couldn't die. Or could they?

Holly stole another look at Myrddin. She had no idea how long he'd been alive. He looked Mr. Smythe's age, except his hair and beard were red not gray. Mr. Smythe was seventy, but Myrddin must be much older. Centuries old? No, thousands of years old. It gave her the shivers to think about it.

Holly closed her eyes. The anxious thoughts milled around and around. At last she too slipped into an uneasy doze.

"Here, try these," Mr. Smythe shouted. He offered Myrddin a pair of headphones and the two-way radio.

Myrddin put them on.

"That's better," said Mr. Smythe's voice in his ear. "Now we can talk without the engine drowning us out."

"Is your dratted machine always this loud?" grumbled Myrddin.

"Now, now! She's singing as sweetly as a bird," said Mr. Smythe with a grin. He patted the control panel.

Myrddin snorted. "We'd have been on Mann in seconds, if we'd gone through the portal."

"But this way we'll arrive without incident," retorted Mr. Smythe, "without your magical friends and enemies conspiring to make life interesting."

"You humans," said Myrddin, "you cannot bring yourself to trust Old Magic."

Mr. Smythe chuckled. "And you cannot bring yourself to trust our planes."

"I have to admit I did not submit willingly. It seems an unnatural mode of locomotion." Myrddin shifted to a more comfortable position in his seat, but his fingers remained clenched on the armrest.

The afternoon sun danced on the sea below, and the sky was a clear pale blue except for a bank of fog hanging on the horizon.

Mr. Smythe pointed. "My instruments tell me the Isle of Man is behind the fogbank." He frowned. "These weather conditions are very strange. The sun is so strong I'd have expected the fog to have burnt off by now."

Myrddin showed no surprise. "Manannan has drawn his cloak of mist around the island. He feels threatened. Zorianna has invaded his kingdom."

Now it was Mr. Smythe's turn to look uneasy. "I hope I am doing the right thing bringing the children here," he muttered.

Adam still slept. Sprawled on the floor and covered with soft wraps, he was deep in the sleep that follows total exhaustion. He turned over. His hand brushed his hair and transferred some Bollan Bane dust to his eyelids. A small dream danced, a silly dream. He saw Owen leaping around trying to catch one of Ava's feathers, only somehow the feather turned into a toothbrush. Adam's lips lifted. He smiled in his sleep, cupped one hand under his cheek and sank into oblivion again.

The Dark Being looked at Adam and also smiled. She found great pleasure planning devious ways to use the boy. As she watched him, she rubbed one finger in a circle on the dark stone in her ring. Round and round she rubbed.

Round and round and round swirled her vortex.

The children woke as the plane circled high above the fog. Mr. Smythe frowned as a voice cackled in his headphones.

He turned his head and hollered to the children over the noise of the engine. "I cannot land yet. The island is socked in with fog. We'll circle for a while. If there are no breaks in the cloud, we might have to go back." He banked and circled again.

The children stared down through the windows.

"I don't see an island. Only sea and fog. How do we know we are flying over the right place?" Chantel asked.

Owen shook his head and pointed to his ears. He could see her lips moving, but he couldn't hear words.

Chantel peered down at the waves and the strange gray mist. She shivered.

Myrddin held up one finger as if to ask for a minute. He leaned back in his seat and closed his eyes.

Owen watched. He nudged Holly, pointed and mouthed, "He's sending mindspeak to someone."

She nodded.

The someone heard Myrddin. They were blasted.
WELCOME.

The stranger's mindspeak was so loud everyone jumped. Along with the greeting flashed a fleeting vision of a white-haired man, arms outstretched, standing on the peak of a heather-covered mountain.

The fog below the plane swirled and parted.

The cousins cheered as they looked down through the gap in the clouds.

A wide swath of sunshine swept across an emerald green island with a spine of purple mountains down the center. It was a pretty place, crisscrossed with stone-walled fields and dotted with white washed cottages. A blue sea frothed against rocky cliffs and headlands on one side of the plane, and, on the other, waves rippled into a wide sandy bay sheltered by a long harbor.

The plane darted down through the gap in the fog.

Chantel laughed. "The island was hiding."

The children pressed their faces against the plane windows.

***

In the maze of passages below the ruins of Peel Castle, Zorianna woke at last and shifted her aching body. She did not know how long she had slept but could sense it was still daylight, though the darkness around her had not lifted.

She lifted her head, checked her wrists and groaned. She'd hoped the staff's magic would wear off. It hadn't. She was still bound from head to foot with thin beams of light. She stared at them. Were the beams fainter?

She tested their strength, jerking her wrists hard apart. The bonds held with the same firm grip.

At least they gave out light. The only light in this terrible place.

Or was it the only light? Zorianna peered into the darkness.

Two sets of eyes glinted. What was staring at her?

Zorianna stared back and made out the faint white shape of a cat.

She curled her lip and dismissed the cat as harmless. She turned her eyes to the thick mass of darkness beside the cat.

Red eyes blinked.

Zorianna shivered, sensing magic and malice. She felt vulnerable, bound and helpless on the floor.

Pressing her back against the dungeon wall, she struggled to stand.

The Moddy Dhoo's eyes blazed.

Zorianna held her head high and glared back.

The dark mass in front of her rose to its feet and growled.

Zorianna forced herself not to flinch.

The cat spoke. "Which do you choose, Light or Dark?"

Relief flooded over her. Zorianna threw back her head and laughed. "Earth Magic is unbelievable! That's it? So simple?"

"Yes, it is quite simple," agreed the cat. "Which do you choose?"

Zorianna chuckled craftily. "Aah...if I choose the Dark, the being I sense at your side will take me. But if I choose Light, you, a cat, will protect me?" She laughed again. "I think not." She thought for a moment. "What if I choose not to make a choice?"

"We will wait," said the cat. "You will choose in the end. You have three chances to choose light."

Zorianna chuckled.

Growling softly, the Moddy Dhoo settled on the ground.

Zorianna tried to stare it down.

The sound of singing interrupted the stalemate.

The song drifted through the castle. The sound was magical, wordless and haunting. Despite its beauty, the voice was filled with a great sadness. The notes sobbed and wailed through the mist and were scattered on the wind.

The song cut through the cries of the restless birds that screamed and wheeled above the castle. It silenced and subdued them. One by one, the gulls returned to the walls where they turned around and around and scratted at their hollows before settling and hiding their heads under their wings.

The eerie voice seeped through cracks in the rocks and echoed along the dark passages and dungeons below.

The sound made Zorianna shiver, for the song held a magic that was not simple. This was Old Magic. Magic she had no wish to challenge.

Zorianna thought about her situation. She was rested, and she could think straight. It was time to make a move while the Earth Magic restraining her remained simple.

Zorianna shape-changed into a bat and tried to slip her bonds.

She was quick, but not quick enough. As she shrank in size so did the bonds. One wing remained pinned to her body.

She changed into water that trickled between the bonds, down the wall and across the floor.

The Moddy Dhoo's red tongue shot out.

Before it reached the water, Zorianna changed into a tiny mouse and ran for a hole in the wall.

Poor choice! The cat pounced. She held the mouse in her mouth. The tail hung from her lips.

"Choose Light or Dark, for the second time of asking," mumbled the cat.

The magical song in the background swelled.

Zorianna turned into a scorpion. One claw grabbed the cat's tongue at the same time as the scorpion tail curled up and stung the cat's nose.

With a yowl of pain the cat opened her mouth and shook her head hard.

The scorpion flew through the air, transforming into a large crab that hit the ground and scuttled toward a crack.

SPLAT. The Moddy Dhoo's paw flattened the crab's body.

AWHOOOOOOoooooo. It was the Black Dog's turn to leap and howl as the crab became a prickly hedgehog that rolled from under the wounded paw and out of sight.

"Earth Magic is so simple," sneered Zorianna and became an owl.

Her owl eyes could see in the dark. She flapped through the labyrinth of tunnels, seeking an exit.

The irritating magical song grew louder.

Light!

A small gap filled with daylight gleamed high up in the dungeon wall. It let in light, a breath of air and the song.

No matter. It offered escape. Zorianna glided toward it.

A thundering, rumbling growl made her shiver.

Something bound past her. The darkness between her and the light thickened.

Zorianna flapped and dodged from side to side searching for a way past.

The Moddy Dhoo's presence grew to fill the space. The light was gone.

Zorianna doubled back.

The white shape of the cat sat in the center of the passage behind her.

"You cannot escape," said the cat.

Zorianna's lip curled. She shape-changed into a black spider invisible in the darkness.

"Very clever," said the cat. "But you cannot escape. Light or Dark, which do you choose?"

The magical song wailed and sobbed.

The spider climbed the dungeon wall.

The cat sighed.

Red eyes gleamed like searchlights.

SPLAT.

The Moddy Dhoo's paw shot out and stunned the spider. Its body tumbled to the floor, stretching, lengthening and returning to the form of a young woman.

Zorianna stirred and opened her eyes.

"Light or Dark? There are no more chances," whispered the cat in her ear. "There is no escape. *'Lhiat myr hoiloo*—to thee as though deservest.' Remember?"

Zorianna remembered and shuddered with fear as the Moddy Dhoo began to bay.

It was a dreadful sound. Each howl rent the air like hundreds of voices shrieking.

The cries swelled around her and brought back terrible memories.

Zorianna remembered every planet she and the Dark Being had visited and destroyed. She heard the cry of each creature she had tormented.

The cries and screams echoed in her head. She writhed

on the floor, blocking her ears. "It wasn't my fault," she screamed. "I just followed orders."

Now laughter rang in her ears. Her own laughter. A cruel laughter echoing back to her from memories of watching Holly and others like her, tormented by mind games of Zorianna's devising.

"Stop it!" shrieked Zorianna. "Stop the cries, stop the voices, stop the laughter."

"I cannot stop it," said the cat. "To thee as thou deservest. They are the voices you unleashed."

The Moddy Dhoo threw back its head, and more terrible howls surrounded them.

Zorianna curled into a ball and stuffed her fingers in her ears. But the howls continued to stir up the cries of terror. Memories of the people she'd hurt filled her head.

Zorianna scrambled to her feet, hands over her ears. Shaking her head from side to side in agony, she stumbled blindly down the corridor.

The Moddy Dhoo bayed on and on.

The cat lifted one paw.

Two silver doorways appeared, one filled with the magical song and brilliant light, one gaping with silent darkness.

Weaving on her feet, Zorianna paused then stumbled into the dark silence.

The cat sighed as the doorways vanished. "She chose the dark."

The Moddy Dhoo blinked and slunk back to his lair.

Remnants of the magical song drifted softly through the air.

Snatches of song floated across the water to Peel town.

In the cottage by the harbor, Mr. Cubbon's deaf ears heard it. He jerked upright at the table, slopping his brew of tea.

"Somethin' startle you?" asked his wife.

"Can yer not hear a maid keening?" said Mr. Cubbon.

"Nay. It's your hearing aid playing its tricks." His wife leaned over and eased it out of his ear. She shook it, gave it a smack and examined the battery.

Mr. Cubbon could still hear the voice.

He watched his wife. She did not hear the sad song. He must be hearing magic sounds. Mr. Cubbon smiled to himself. It was his special gift come back again. In childhood he'd heard things. Things no one else heard. "Me magic ear," he'd called it to himself. He'd never spoken of it, and it had died away as he grew up. Now in his old age, his magic ear was back. He might be deaf to many everyday sounds, but his magic ear enriched his life. He was content to be called eccentric when folks heard him holding conversations with shadows on the beach, the raven, or the sprite that lived in Spooyt Vane. No one dreamed that he really did see spirits and understand animals and birds.

Mr. Cubbon supped his tea and made no further mention of the song. But he wondered what this new stirring of sad magic would bring.

The song drifted to and fro, up and down the narrow streets of Peel. No other person had ears that heard it. The notes crept into cracks and crevices, echoed down gratings and into the long forgotten smuggler's passages that ran under the sea, linking Pheric's Isle to Peel.

The song rippled through the still air in the passages, stirring centuries of dust that had collected on an old oak board leaning against the wall. The dust dropped away and revealed ancient scratchings on the wooden surface.

The song sighed into silence.

CHAPTER FIVE

A CIRCLING OF SHADES

Ava's flight toward the vortex was a struggle. She panted and gasped, and her tiny body trembled with effort.

I must not use magic. I must not use magic, she told herself. I must be as a speck of dust, unnoticed unless it irritates an eye!

Ava forced her wings to beat slowly and steadily, to disturb nothing, to draw no attention her way.

The constant swirling of the Shades made the pull of the vortex remorseless. It dragged at her, sucking her toward its center.

Ava tried to keep control, making her wings beat harder and deeper. Forcing her body to resist the force.

One more circle should be enough, she thought. One more...timed just right.

Her body began to shake uncontrollably.

The pull was almost more than she could bear.

NOW!

Ava opened her beak and dropped the feather and hair.

Almost invisible, they were swept toward the black center.

Ava didn't stay to watch. She turned, beating her tiny wings as hard as she could.

The vortex held her fast. Her strength was gone.

Ava drifted toward the void.

PAIN. A bite of agonizing pain.

One wing tip had brushed the edge of the dark shadow.

In a last attempt to free herself, Ava folded her wings against her body and thrust her head down into a dive, away from the dark.

For a second, everything hung in balance. Ava's body was held suspended.

She gave a massive jerk, broke the hold of the vortex and plummeted down through the stars toward the sunbeam shielding Equus.

The small floatplane circled several times above the Isle of Man as Mr. Smythe requested landing clearance from Peel harbor authorities.

Chantel stared in fascination at the waves breaking against the headland below.

Myrddin had said this was a magic island, and he was right. Among the white frothy wave tops she spotted tossing heads and the streaming manes of white horses. They reared up, exposing their forelegs, and sank back into the sea again. They were the horses from her dream. She laughed and nudged Owen. "Look at the white horses," she shouted.

Owen smiled at her description of the waves. "Good job it's sheltered in the bay," he shouted back, "or we couldn't land."

Chantel subsided.

She watched the waves again. The horses were there, as plain as plain, dozens of them! She wasn't dreaming, but Owen hadn't seen them. Holly had said nothing about the horses either. She must be the only one who could see them. What did it mean?

Holly ignored the sea. She stared at the land. She'd spotted a road, a causeway, joining what must have been an islet to the main island. The islet contained a ruined castle and within its walls she'd glimpsed a tall round tower.

The castle seemed strangely familiar. With a jolt, Holly remembered a fragment of a dream...She'd seen this castle before. With a second jolt she recognized the tower, but it disappeared before she got a clear view.

Holly pressed her face to the window and crossed her fingers, willing the plane to circle over the headland again.

YES! It soared directly over the ruined castle, and there was the tower again. It was the round tower from her vision, with the strange door built high up in the wall and no steps to reach it.

Everything had changed. This was no longer the bleak rocky isle in the past, but she was sure it was the same place. She stared down.

Suddenly she felt Breesha.

Breesha pulled at her heart as surely as if her invisible hand was tugging on Holly's arm.

The hair on the back of Holly's neck prickled, and the bead in her pocket seemed hard and heavy. Breesha's grave was down there, somewhere within the castle walls, and she must find it and somehow return the bead!

Cool place, thought Owen as he looked down. He liked ruined castles. He loved exploring them and imagining they belonged to him. He could see inside this one. There were walkways along the walls and even a row of cannons. Cool. In one area people seemed to be digging, but the plane flew past before he could see more.

Hundreds of birds wheeled in the air between the castle and the plane. Owen watched the nearest gull soaring effortlessly and was vividly reminded of flying with Ava the Hawkwoman, over the stone circle at Avebury. His mind flooded with anxiety. Something was wrong with Ava. He could sense it. She was scared! Why was a Wise One scared?

Owen looked over to Myrddin to see if he was picking up the same feeling.

Myrddin's eyes were closed and his hands gripped the armrest. Owen couldn't tell why.

Owen closed his eyes and sent mindspeak to his favorite

Wise One. *Ava, what's wrong? Where are you? Do you need help?*

The Dark Being stopped fingering her ring. With an impatient movement of her arm she gestured to the Shades to cease circling and close the vortex. There was no point wasting energy the Shades would need for the final confrontation.

"Gather along the fringes of the Mists of Time," she ordered. "It cannot repel forever. Others use the Mists and will wish to enter. Be poised, ready to slip through any break. Then go to Gaia and spy on the humans. Watch for magical activities that might lead us to Myrddin's staff. Be silent. Be stealthy. Gather information and enjoy making the humans uncomfortable and angry. Once I have what I seek, I will join you with the rest of my forces. Then I will reward you."

She was so intent on giving orders that she didn't notice a tiny hair and feather drop into the gray stillness.

To and fro...to and fro...to and fro...the feather drifted... slowly the hair uncurled and separated.

The white hair floated down and caught in the Dark Being's wild mane, causing a tiny spark of white light. There it lay, a single thread of white entangled in the black.

The Dark Being tossed her head and went on with her invasion plans. The movement made the tiny feather swirl again.

It circled lower and lower and touched the cheek of the sleeping child. Once again it gave off a minute spark.

Without waking, Adam brushed his face with his hand, trapping the feather between his palm and cheek. He turned over.

Equus tensed as, without warning, the vortex closed. Had it caught Ava?

He felt two tiny jolts and he knew the feather and hair had reached their destination. For good or bad they had forged a connection with the Dark Being.

Ava did not reappear.

Equus waited and waited, growing more anxious with each passing minute.

At last he spotted her.

Something was wrong. Ava wasn't flying, she was tumbling, her wing beats jerky and ineffective.

Equus sent a cocoon of light to cushion her.

Ava managed a weak "thank you" and sprawled on his back.

Equus resumed the journey to Gaia, checking on Ava every few minutes. "The cost of your journey was great. Was it too great a price to pay?" he asked.

"The Darkness...," Ava struggled to answer him. "The Darkness touched me."

Equus shuddered. Ava had paid a price indeed. The dark touch would creep through her, in time freezing both mind and body.

"Ava, keep Light in your heart. We will heal you. I will take you straight to the Lady's resting place, the most powerful place on Gaia," called out Equus. "We will surround you with light, Earth Magic and Old Magic."

Ava could not answer.

With a great leap Equus entered the edges of the Mists of Time. They pushed back against him, refusing entry.

"Newly charged Mists of Time, I welcome you back and request your help," he called out. "We are Equus and Ava, two Wise Ones you once knew well. We require safe passage to Gaia. Myrddin will vouch for us."

The Mists chattered amongst themselves, thinned for a moment, and thickened on Equus's heels as he passed through.

They thickened fast, but not fast enough.

Several Shades slid through in Equus's wake.

⬡⬡⬡

Mr. Smythe's headphone crackled. He gave everyone a thumbs-up. The little plane darted through the gap in the clouds, toward the calm water in the bay.

The plane dropped lower and lower. Mr. Smythe throttled back and touched down gently. There was a great splash, then the Beaver coasted along the surface of the water. Turning in a wide circle she putted toward the harbor and turned into the river estuary. Mr. Smythe cut the engine. The plane drifted to a stop by a large orange buoy bobbing in a patch of brilliant sunshine.

"Our thanks, Manannan, for a safe arrival," said Myrddin with a heartfelt sigh of relief.

Mr. Smythe snorted.

The children's eyes danced. They hid giggles.

Mr. Smythe swung out of the cockpit door and stood on the float. He tied up to the buoy.

Holly raised her eyebrows.

"Er...it's a long way to swim to the harbor steps," shouted Owen.

Mr. Smythe pointed to the quay. "The harbor master's sending a rowboat. Peel doesn't have a floatplane dock, and we cannot tie up beside the harbor. We'd damage our wings."

"Got it," said Owen. He watched a rowboat leave the steps and approach them. The oarsman expertly maneuvered among the anchored pleasure boats and fishing boats.

"Afternoon, all. Mr. Cubbon at your service. I'll take the kiddies first," shouted the fisherman with confidence. He shipped the oars, pushed up the sleeves of his thick navy blue sweater and held the boat steady against the floats. "Come on. She's quite safe."

"You're nearest the door. Climb out first, Owen," instructed Mr. Smythe. "Come down the ladder to the float and hang on to a strut. Holly, you help Chantel down, and Owen and I will grab her. Myrddin, sit tight and balance the weight. We'll go next with the luggage."

It took some time for the three children to disembark from the plane, balance on the float and clamber into the rowboat, but everyone managed without falling into the water.

"Super cool," said Owen as they left the rowboat and scrambled up the harbor steps. He stared around with interest.

The flapping corner of a poster caught his eye.

Peel Viking Festival it announced. *WANTED: Volunteers for the role of Vikings to re-enact a raid on Peel castle.*

Owen's eyes shone. Now that was the sort of thing he would love to do. Pity they had other things on their minds. As he scanned the harbor he spotted replicas of the dragon-prowed Viking longboats, bobbing among the fishing vessels.

"Look at the Viking longboats. After this is over, do you think we'll be able to cadge a ride in one?" he asked.

Chantel and Holly didn't answer.

Holly stared at the castle at the end of the causeway.

Chantel leaned over the far side of the causeway wall, watching the breaking waves.

"I'd love to be part of the Viking raid," said Owen. He stared wistfully at the longboats, then turned his attention to the fishing village of Peel on the other side of the estuary. "We must be staying over there," he said, pointing at the rows of stone cottages that lined winding streets. "Which do you think is our hotel?"

Chantel joined him, but Holly never turned her head. She wasn't interested in boats; she wasn't interested in the town of Peel. She needed to find Breesha's grave and she needed to find it soon.

AARCK.

A lone raven soared above her and disappeared over the castle walls.

I call upon the raven to guide her. Sigurd's words at Breesha's graveside echoed in Holly's mind. If the raven was a guide, she should follow it. Holly began to run.

"Hey up, Holly. Wait for Mr. Smythe and Myrddin," protested Owen.

"They'll see us. It's not far. Come on. Follow the raven," Holly shouted.

Surprised, Owen and Chantel looked at each other, then across the water to the plane. Mr. Cubbon had rowed back out, and the adults were struggling to unloaded luggage from the rear of the plane into his boat.

"OY! Mr. Smythe!" hollered Owen.

Mr. Smythe turned. The rowboat wobbled, and he lunged forward and grabbed the float. He steadied himself, turned again and shook his fist.

Owen grinned. He cupped his hands to his mouth. "We'll wait by the castle," he yelled and pointed.

Mr. Smythe raised a hand in agreement and turned back to the plane.

"Right. Now we're off the hook!" Owen said, grinning.

The two cousins raced down the causeway after Holly.

❈❈❈

AARK, cried the raven. He stared down from the red sandstone battlements above the castle gatehouse.

Holly stared up. "What are you trying to tell me?" she called.

With a creak of wings, a second bird swooped down to join him. They rubbed beaks and watched the girl with two sets of beady eyes.

"Your mate is a white raven. That's really rare!" Holly's voice was full of awe. "Light and Dark, Dark and Light. You're a pair of magical birds."

The white raven hopped along the battlement to be

closer to the girl. The bird tilted her head to one side, then the other, spread her wings and flew back inside the castle.

AARK. The black raven followed.

"So? What's the hurry? Why did you rush off?" panted Owen as he and Chantel caught up with Holly.

Holly pointed up the worn steps, through the gatehouse, to the castle's pay booth. "Did you bring any money? We need it to go inside."

"Hold on, Holly," Owen protested. "We've only just arrived. What's the big rush?"

Holly calmed down a little. "I recognize this place. It's where Breesha's buried. I must get inside. The round tower I saw in my vision is in the middle of the castle. So's Breesha. I can feel her pulling me."

"Magic's pulling me too," admitted Chantel softly. "Myrddin said we were coming to the most magical place on earth. He was right. The sea is full of white horses."

Owen grinned and ruffled her hair. "You and your horses."

Chantel moved out of reach, her face set.

"Nothing's calling me," said Owen. "But this is a brilliant place to visit. The only thing I feel is worried about Ava. I'm scared she's in big trouble."

Everyone fell silent. They had still heard nothing from the other two Wise Ones.

A white cat poked its head through a window slit in the gatehouse. It saw the children, jumped down and wound around their ankles.

Chantel stooped and stroked it. "Oh...a white cat...I dreamed about one like you.... What a nice welcome, pretty kitty." She ran her hand along its body. "Ooops, you've no tail. You must be a Manx cat. That makes you special." Chantel scooped the cat up and rubbed her cheek against the soft fur. "I'll call you Manxie," she crooned.

The cat purred.

"Ooooh, you like that name. Look at Manxie, everyone."

Holly tickled behind the cat's ears.

The cat stretched and turned in Chantel's arms, offering up its soft belly.

Owen chuckled and joined in, stroking and petting the beautiful animal.

A voice began to sing.

The sound floated over the castle walls.

The children's hands stilled as they listened.

The cat twisted out of Chantel's arms, leapt back up the wall and melted through the window slit.

The song continued. It sobbed its way into the children's hearts. Tears pooled in their eyes.

Holly sensed that the song was trying to tell her something, but she couldn't grasp the words.

"How awful, having no one remember your name," said Chantel with a sigh. She sniffed.

The others stared at her.

"What on earth are you talking about?" said Holly.

"The singer who has no name," said Chantel in surprise.

Holly grabbed her arm. "You mean you understand the song?"

"Sure, don't you?"

"No, I just hear sad sounds," said Holly.

"That's all I hear," said Owen, "so how could you hear words? You're making it up."

Chantel flushed. "Get lost, Owen. You never believe me. You're as bad as Adam." The thought of Adam brought more tears to her eyes. She turned away.

Mr. Smythe, Myrddin and Mr. Cubbon emerged one by one up the harbor steps. Chantel ran back to them.

"Idiot," said Holly to Owen. "Now look what you've done. I know she's only seven, but she's got magic we don't have. Equus said Chantel was the Singer, remember? She might be hearing something we can't, and now she's mad at us."

Owen kicked a broken scallop shell. "Sorry," he muttered. "But she's getting more fanciful since Adam disappeared. I'm trying to keep her grounded." He sighed. "I'll apologize. She'll get over it."

"She'd better," said Holly. "Something tells me I really need to understand that song." She turned and followed Chantel.

Chantel reached Mr. Smythe as he stood catching his breath.

Holly and Owen saw her gesturing toward the castle.

The men turned their heads to look.

Holly speeded up to join them. "Mr. Cubbon, do you know who's singing?" she panted.

"Singing? It's more like sobbing," said Owen, coming up behind.

"What singing?" Mr. Smythe tilted his head to listen.

He shrugged. "I don't hear a thing."

The children looked baffled. The song was faint but still clear.

Mr. Cubbon said nothing. He stared hard at each child from under his shaggy brows.

Myrddin looked mysterious.

Holly opened her mouth as if to say more, but Owen nudged her. "Shhhh. If no one else hears it, it must be magic music," he whispered and indicated Mr. Cubbon.

Holly snapped her mouth shut.

A fierce gust of wind whooshed in from the sea, bobbing and tossing boats at their moorings. It carried a frantic galloping of hooves.

A portal, Manannan. We pray you a portal, and your help.

The urgent mindspeak startled everyone.

All four children's heads whipped around. Mr. Smythe, Myrddin and Mr. Cubbon also turned.

The flag above the gatehouse leapt and billowed, then dropped and lay idle again as the gust passed.

The strange wind gusted across the causeway, up the headland and into the hills beyond. The hoofbeats faded.

"It's Equus," cried Chantel. "He's in trouble."

"Not him...Ava," said Owen grimly. He turned to Mr. Smythe. "We've got to help them. Sir."

No one argued. The blast of mindspeak was full of dread and foreboding.

Another buffet of wind followed.

The mist boiled and closed in again, but not before

strange shadows raced over the water, along the harbor and across the headland.

Everyone shivered as the shadows passed.

"Oh, for my staff, my staff," muttered Myrddin under his breath.

Chantel overheard. She slipped her hand in his and squeezed.

"Aye, strange doings. Magical doings," murmured Mr. Cubbon as threads of mist swirled around and between them again. "Manannan's drawin' his cloak around his island. Summat's threatening his kingdom."

The entire group stared in surprise at the old fisherman.

It was Chantel who got straight to the heart of the matter. She touched Mr. Cubbon's arm. "You heard Equus, didn't you?" she said.

Mr. Cubbon nodded. "The White Horse, aye."

"...and the magic song?"

Mr. Cubbon nodded again.

"Did you understand the words?"

"Aye. 'Twas the old story of the spirit whose name is lost. She cannot rest till someone remembers it."

Holly sucked in her breath.

"Told ya," sang out Chantel. She turned back to Mr. Cubbon. "Were you a Magic Child?" she asked.

Mr. Cubbon's face broke into a delighted smile. "No one ever called me that, me dear. But me Magic Ear was wondrous when I was a child. And 'tis wondrous again of late. I'm thinking we should get you set up at Castleview Inn. Then if I was you, I'd head to Barrule."

"Barrule?" the children murmured.

"Aye, the mountain where Manannan lives. The direction yon White Horse was galloping. Seems like you have urgent need of Manannan. Come along now. I borrowed the fishmonger's van to carry the luggage." Mr. Cubbon began to haul a couple of backpacks toward a white minivan, parked farther down the quay, barely visible through the now dense fog.

He didn't notice a strange dark shadow following him.

<hr>

The Shade sent out a cry to other shades. "Humans sspeak of magic. I will sstay sstay, and lissten lissten."

It shadowed Mr. Cubbon, puddling beneath his feet as he climbed into the driver's seat of the van.

Mr. Cubbon shivered and pulled down the sleeves of his sweater as the temperature around him plummeted.

CHAPTER SIX

Magical Secrets

It was a short drive to the Castleview Inn, one of the old buildings Owen had spotted on the other side of the harbor.

Built from stone like the castle, but whitewashed and brightly painted with red trim, the inn rambled unevenly alongside the estuary of the river Nebb.

Despite the foggy gloom, flower baskets on either side of the door made for a cheery mood.

Holly entered the room she was sharing with Chantel, dumped her backpack on the bed and ran to the windows. She gave a sigh of relief. She could just see the castle across the estuary. The walls floated fairy-like through the mist. She pushed open the window and listened. The magical singing had ceased.

"Brrr," said Chantel pointedly and pulled on a sweater.

Holly shut the window. "Chantel," she said, "this place oozes magic. I think we should try to use it."

Chantel stopped unpacking. She stared at Holly. "How?"

"Well, we all mindspeak with the Wise Ones, but have you ever tried to mindspeak with one of us when we are not doing magic?" Holly asked.

Chantel shook her head. Her eyes widened. "No. I never thought of it."

"Me neither," said Holly. "But I've been thinking—what if we can? We're Magic Children in the most magical place on earth. We are challenging the Dark Being, and it would be really useful to mindspeak or mind read among ourselves."

Chantel nodded and sat crosslegged on the bed. "Okay, let's try."

Holly perched on the radiator. "I'll think about an object, and you tell me what it is." She closed her eyes.

Chantel closed hers and concentrated, frowning with the effort.

"Err...a ball...a bead. Are you thinking about the black bead?" she asked, bouncing in her excitement.

Holly grinned and nodded. "Your turn."

Both girls closed their eyes.

Holly was quicker. "You're thinking about the cat," she said.

Chantel's eyes shone. "Wow! Let's try mindspeak."

They both took deep breaths and closed their eyes.

Are you there, Chantel?

I'm here.

What's black and white and read all over?

Chantel giggled. *That's an old one. A newspaper.* She opened her eyes. "Brilliant, Holly. Let's see if we can do it with Owen."

"And Adam," said Holly quietly.

Chantel gasped.

"But don't get your hopes up. We need to check it out. Maybe we can only do it when we're both concentrating." Holly laughed. "And we should find out how to block it. I don't want you knowing my innermost secrets."

Chantel shot her a wicked look. "Me neither."

"We'll check with Myrddin before trying to reach Adam. I don't fancy talking to the Dark Being!" Holly slid off the radiator. "But I need to sort out Mr. Smythe first."

Chantel frowned.

"I don't care what he thinks, he can't stop us talking to Myrddin, and I can't mess around going to Barrule. It's daft." She rummaged in her backpack, found her fanny pack, checked for money and clipped the pack around her waist. "I'm going to the castle. Coming, Chantel?"

Without waiting for an answer Holly strode out to tackle Mr. Smythe.

Chantel stayed on the bed, staring at the door. "Please don't fight with Mr. Smythe, Holly," she murmured. "I hate it when people fight."

⁂

Mr. Smythe and Myrddin stood beside the table, looking down at a map of the Isle of Man. They were arguing.

"There is the mountain Barrule." Myrddin tapped his

finger on the map. "It's Manannan's home and where we'll find Equus and Ava. Of course I'll use magic."

"No magic. It's unnecessary," insisted Mr. Smythe. "I'll hire a car and drive you."

Holly marched up to them.

Mr. Smythe looked up. "Ah, Holly, you're ready."

Holly shook her head.

"Not me. Sorry Mr. Smythe, I'm going to the castle," she said firmly. "And I need to talk to Myrddin first."

Mr. Smythe's face froze.

Holly tried to soften her tone. "I know you're trying to protect us, but it's impossible."

"That's what I said," snorted Myrddin.

"I did magic while you were on the phone this morning, Mr. Smythe," continued Holly. "Now I need to talk to Myrddin about it, because if I don't ask his advice I might do something dangerous. We all need to talk. We mustn't keep any more secrets from each other."

She turned to Myrddin while Mr. Smythe struggled for words.

"I had a vision, Myrddin," said Holly urgently. "I saw someone being buried, and her grave is calling to me. It's in the castle. I need to find it."

Myrddin was transfixed. "You witnessed a burial on Pheric's Isle?"

Holly nodded. "Yes, a woman called Breesha." She pulled the black bead out of her pocket. "This belongs to her."

Myrddin paled. He put his hands behind his back and retreated. "You're right, Holly. We should have discussed this earlier...If that is what I think it is..." Myrddin seemed lost for words. "Put it away. Handle it as little as possible." He waited until Holly had tucked the bead back in her pocket. "How is it in your possession?"

"Breesha had a necklace...it was fabulous...with all different beads, turquoise, and amber..."

"And jet," said Myrddin. His voice was strained.

"Yes. This jet bead was on it. The necklace was broken by accident at the burial, and the beads scattered..."

Myrddin grew even paler and sat down with a bump at the table. "This explains everything. Go on, child. What happened to the beads?"

"The women gathered them up and replaced them, propping them back around Breesha's neck. They tried to put them in the right order, but this one had rolled and they missed it. I found it after the burial was complete and everyone had left."

"One little bead. That was all it took. One little bead of immense importance. It is the Dark Being's bead. This is how she has grown so powerful. She is no longer influenced by the necklace. And the broken string no longer binds the magic of the worlds together." Myrddin's head sank into his hands. His muffled voice was full of sadness.

"Was...was Breesha the Lady?" asked Holly fearfully.

"That was a name given to her when she last visited Gaia clothed in an earthly body," said Myrddin heavily. "Just as I have taken a human form and go by the name Mervin Green in my current life on Gaia."

"Bu...but, then is the Lady...really dead?" whispered Holly.

Myrddin roused himself. "No...no, she isn't dead," he said. "Her earthly body died, but instead of becoming a Wise One again, she chose to become the Sleeper, ready to wake when needed. But she didn't know her necklace would break. She cannot wake while the necklace is broken and incomplete."

Holly stared at him in horror, her hand clamped over her pocket. "We must fix it! Can you do it?"

Myrddin shook his head. He was still slumped at the table. "Everything is in jeopardy because that tiny bead was lost...," he whispered. A long moment passed before he straightened, his jaw set. "Holly, once again Earth Magic is seeking you out. You are right. You *must* go to the castle and follow your instincts. Keep the bead safe, my child. Repair the necklace."

"How?" cried Holly. "It was buried with Breesha."

"Trust in Earth Magic. One bead has already come your way." Myrddin turned to Mr. Smythe.

"Let her go, Smythe. Earth Magic has chosen. Without the Lady's necklace the entire universe is lost."

Mr. Smythe fidgeted. He ignored Myrddin. "It's dangerous," he said to Holly. "I'll accompany you."

Myrddin's eyes flashed.

Holly drew herself up. "Mr. Smythe, I'm not a kid. I'm nearly twelve years old. I do lots of things on my own, and right now I have to go to that castle. Even if you were with me, you couldn't do anything. You're not a Magic Child, and you can't stop the magic! And I'm sorry, because this sounds rude...but you might get in the way."

"That's what I've told him," said Myrddin.

Mr. Smythe's voice was desperate. "I must look after you. I have to answer to your parents. I'm responsible for you."

His words hung in the air. Both Myrddin and Holly knew the unspoken words were, "You must not disappear like Adam."

Holly's back softened. Her anger left her. "It's not your fault. You can't stop the magic," she repeated softly. "No one can stop it now."

"She's right," said Myrddin.

Mr. Smythe glared.

Holly smiled patiently, suddenly seeming older and wiser than her years. "Mr. Smythe, please understand. We're not disobeying you. We're compelled to follow the magic. Ask Myrddin. He'll tell you."

"I've told him, a dozen times," muttered Myrddin.

Holly touched Mr. Smythe's arm. "I think there's a reason why you're with us, Mr. Smythe. I think Earth Magic has a job for you. You helped us find the Red Mare in the first adventure, and you taught us about the Spiral Labyrinth at Glastonbury in the last adventure. I think we'll need your skills again."

Mr. Smythe gave a small smile. His eyes were tired. "Thank you, Holly. You know I'll help with anything I can." He ran his hands through his hair.

"Then help us now by accepting Myrddin's magic. You've been afraid to let us alone with him. But we need him, his magic and his advice," Holly said urgently.

There was a long silence.

"Myrddin, will Holly be safe in the castle on her own?" said Mr. Smythe.

Myrddin's eyebrows shot together. "She'll be safe going to the castle. She'll be safe looking around. But you're asking me if she will be safe from magic...Of course not. None of them will. They're Magic Children," he roared.

Holly chuckled.

Mr. Smythe gave in. "Holly, I apologize. I can't stop the magic, and of course you need Myrddin's advice."

Holly and Myrddin exchanged smiles.

"Thank you, Mr. Smythe," said Holly.

Mr. Smythe stretched wearily and looked around. "Where are Chantel and Owen?"

"Chantel's in the bedroom, and Owen's in the cellar," said Holly. "While you were registering, the landlord and Mr. Cubbon told him about smugglers' passages that run under Peel. There's supposed to be one hidden in the Castleview Inn's cellar. Owen's trying to find it."

Mr. Smythe threw up his hands. "I give up. There's always something. I'll go and find him while you talk with Myrddin."

Mr. Smythe opened the door and walked down the corridor. "Owen...Owen, where are you?"

Chantel heard the raised voices within seconds of Holly leaving the bedroom. She flung herself across the bed and pulled the pillow over her ears. "I hate arguing. Hate it, hate it, hate it!" she muttered into the quilt.

She felt sick. Sick of worrying about Adam. Sick of being yelled at by her mother. Sick of Holly and Owen not believing what she was seeing or hearing. Chantel lifted one side of the pillow. She could still hear arguments. She muffled her ears again, wishing she had a magic wand to make everything all right. They needed Myrddin's wand, his magic staff. If they found that it would help everyone. Myrddin would have his full powers back.

Chantel rolled on her back and gazed up at the ceiling.

Here she was in the Isle of Man. So was Myrddin's staff; he'd said so. Adam couldn't get it because he was captured. What if she could find it? Then Myrddin could magic everything all right.

Chantel closed her eyes tight and tried out her new skill at mindspeak. *Er...Manannan...are you there? It's me...Chantel...I'm Adam's sister. I'm a Magic Child too.* She held her breath.

Welcome, Chantel. Manannan hears you.

Chantel received a similar mind picture to the one she'd seen on the plane. A white-haired old man stood listening on the heather-clad slopes of a mountain she now knew was Barrule.

She sat up and tried to gather her thoughts.

Manannan, we need help.

I know child. The Darkness deepens. Even the people of Mann grow restless and irritable.

We need Myrddin's staff. I think you know where it is.

I do.

Can you get it?

No. Only the Myrddin can handle his staff. Or someone chosen by him.

Could a Magic Child get it?

That is the simplest way.

Adam can't. He was the Magic Child chosen by Myrddin, but he's been caught. We need the staff to help him.

That is correct, child.

I'm a Magic Child too. Could I get it?

You could. The staff is safe. It lies where Zorianna discarded it, within the secret passages 'neath Pheric's Castle. If you have the courage to face those who reside there, the staff will allow the touch of a Magic Child. But you must never wield it. Only the Myrddin can wield his staff.

How do I go to the passages?

Like this...

Chantel heard Manannan take a deep breath and blow.

The bedroom filled with a whirling wind that surrounded, lifted and swept her away.

The wind set her down gently.

Everything was black. Ahh, her eyes were closed. Chantel opened them. Everything was still black.

She shivered. It was one thing to have an idea. It was quite another to carry it out.

She didn't dare move, not knowing what was around her. She stood still in the endless darkness.

She became aware of sounds, normal sounds. First, she heard waves in the distance. They pounded and hissed regularly as though beating against rock. They reminded her of a dream that had brought comfort. Chantel smiled slightly. "Hello, Gaia's heartbeat," she whispered. Her fear receded a little—water was part of the Lady's magic.

Her heart lightened.

The second sound she identified was more water. It dripped as though from the roof of a cave or passage and she became aware of the walls of rock around her, enclosing her, but also protecting her and providing a firm foundation for her feet.

The muffled cries of gulls also brought comfort. She knew where she was now, in a passage beneath the castle on Pheric's Isle. She pictured the gulls wheeling above the walls.

Chantel breathed more easily. She was surrounded by three symbols of Earth Magic, and if she kept light in her heart, she had the fourth.

"I must remember the light," she whispered. Her words echoed softly down the passage. "I must remember the light," she said again, more firmly. "Earth is below me, water is around me, air is above me and I hold light in my heart."

On the floor in front of her, a tiny gleam broke the darkness.

Chantel bent and picked it up. It was a hair, a glowing white hair: a tiny light in a great dark. She held it high.

"I have light," she said, confidently.

"You chose light," a voice answered. A white shape moved toward her.

"Manxie." Chantel held out her arms, and the cat leapt into them. "You're part of the light. You're part of Earth Magic."

"I am Earth Magic." The cat purred and nuzzled her

cheek. "And you have chosen to follow the light. Keep my hair. You may use it again. Come, follow me."

"All right," said Chantel, joy in her voice.

"You will have to let me go," said the cat with a slight sniff.

Chantel chuckled and relaxed her arms.

The cat sprang down and walked ahead, her fur's soft light illuminating the passage.

Chantel followed through the twists and turns of the secret way.

The cat sat. "We are here."

"Where?" said Chantel.

"At the place where Zorianna discarded the staff."

Chantel shuddered. "I don't want to meet Zorianna."

"She's not here," said the cat dismissively. "Only the staff."

Chantel peered into the darkness. She saw nothing.

"The staff is hiding. You must find it."

"Staff," Chantel called, not knowing what else to do, "I'm a Magic Child, a friend of Myrddin's. I've come to take you back to him."

Nothing stirred.

Chantel tried again. "Staff, Adam unlocked you from the Crystal Cave. I'm his sister, Chantel."

No response.

Chantel considered the problem. She needed Earth Magic to locate the staff. She didn't have water or a candle or anything to do a ritual. The only thing she could use was her voice. Equus had said it was her magic tool.

She tried Holly's chant.

"Earth support me,
Air surround me,

Fire enlighten me,
Water cleanse me."

"Earth support me,
Air surround me,
Fire enlighten me,
Water cleanse me."

The darkness lightened slightly, a feeling of peace surrounded her, but the staff did not betray its presence.

Chantel tried again. She voiced the chant they had learned in Avebury.

"Light and Dark, Dark and Light,
Sun by day, Moon by night,
Man and woman, adult, child,
Bird and beast both tame and wild,
Past and present, far and near,
Patience, anger, hope and fear,
Frantic movement, contemplation,
The Dance of Stones, a celebration!" she finished.

The cat purred and wove around her ankle.

The staff remained hidden.

"Nothing's working, Manxie," said Chantel. "Equus is my Wise One, not Myrddin. I don't know how to call things for Myrddin. Oh, Equus, I wish you were here to help." She tried sending mindspeak. *Please, Equus, talk to me. Can't you help? Can't you hear me?*

Silence.

What's wrong with everyone? Talk to me, Equus. I know you've gone to Barrule. I heard you galloping there.

More silence.

Chantel stamped in frustration. She sent out a general blast of mindspeak.

Equus, Ava, Myrddin, Manannan...Please...someone answer me?

I am the only one who can hear, Child. A web protects Pheric's Isle's magic realm. Only my magic can freely flow through it.

Manannan. Thank goodness! Can you help me?

I can try, Child. What is your need?

How do I call Myrddin's staff?

I have heard Myrddin call up his magic with a verse. Try it, Child, then use your own words.

A talisman to hone the mind,
A circlet old to hold and bind,
A staff to smite with hidden might,
Beads to link and hold the light.

Thank you, Manannan! Thank you. Chantel sent a wave of gratitude and returned to her task.

She began to chant...

"A talisman to hone the mind,

A circlet old to hold and bind,

A staff to smite with hidden might,

Beads to link and hold the light...

In Myrddin's name I call you, staff. Myrddin needs you. Please let me take you to him."

The staff flew out of the darkness, its tip shining like a shooting star.

Chantel's hand shot up and caught it. The staff shook and quivered at her touch, and settled into the crook of her arm.

"Thank you, Manannan. And thank you, Manxie, for bringing me here." Chantel bent to stroke the cat. "Can we go back to Myrddin now?"

A loud rumbling growl startled her.

The cat sat.

"Is that a dog?" Chantel peered through the darkness.

The growl rumbled again, and two red eyes blinked at Chantel's knee level.

"You're a very black dog," said Chantel. "I can't see your body at all." She chuckled. "You must be as dark as the darkness."

She heard a faint sound as though a large furry animal was stirring. A scrabble of claws on rock sounded as though it was rising to its feet. The eyes blinked again, this time level with Chantel's head.

The growl was a loud ominous rumble.

"Goodness," said Chantel. "You're humongous. Why are you so scared of me?" she chuckled. "You shouldn't be. I'm just a kid, and you're so big." She paused as she remembered something Holly had told her. "Are you the Black Dog that helps protect the Lady? The one Holly heard in her dream?"

The growl died away. The darkness stirred and snuffled.

"Here, dog, smell me." Chantel held out her free hand.

"I'm a friend. I'm one of the Magic Children come to help the Lady. I'm taking Myrddin's staff back to him."

A cold nose sniffed Chantel's hand. A wet lick followed.

Chantel laughed and dried off her hand on her pants.

"I've never seen that before," said the cat stiffly. "He'll be turning white if he's not careful. Come!" She stood, skirted around the Moddy Dhoo and resumed her journey.

Chantel followed but kept turning to look. She could sense the Moddy Dhoo padding at her heels, but he stayed blended with the dark.

Finally the cat stopped. "This was your place of arrival, child, so it is your place of departure. Remember, you may need my light again."

Chantel stroked the cat's head. "Thanks for your help, Manxie. I'd have been really scared without you."

A low whine sounded behind her. Chantel turned and put out her hand. "Thank you too, Black Dog. I'm glad we made friends. I'll tell Myrddin you're still protecting the Lady." She felt rough fur against her palm and patted it.

Manannan, are you there? I have the staff.

So I see. There was amusement in Manannan's voice. *You chose the Light and tamed the Dark. You have useful talents, child.*

Chantel smiled, not sure what he meant. *I like dogs and cats. I like all ani...*

The wind blew and swirled her away.

She landed with a bump in the bedroom.

Chantel walked into the living area. "Here—stop arguing everyone." She held out the staff to Myrddin.

CHAPTER SEVEN

FRIENDS AND ENEMIES

Myrddin and Holly stopped talking and stared at Chantel.

Chantel was no longer the worried waif from the morning. She beamed from ear to ear as she held the staff.

Myrddin gave a roar of delight. He leapt out the chair, enfolded Chantel in a gigantic hug and stretched out his arm.

With a spit and a crack, the staff leapt toward him. The crystal at the tip sparked with the fiery light of a magnificent diamond as the shaft slammed into his palm.

Myrddin seemed to grow. His red hair and beard crackled with static electricity. His dark cloak swirled with the million hidden colors of magic. The Myrddin was whole again.

"Myrddin's st—staff was in our bedroom? I don't believe it!" stuttered Holly.

Chantel emerged laughing from the tangle of cloak, staff and beard. "You should see your face." She went into a fit of giggles, but shook her head. "Course it wasn't in the bedroom. I did what you said, Holly. I did mindspeak and Earth Magic while you were all arguing. I spoke to Manannan, and he took me to the secret passages where the staff was hiding. The white cat showed me the way. The staff let me hold it, and I made friends with a big black dog. Manannan brought me back."

"Just like that?" said Holly.

"Pretty much," said Chantel.

Myrddin laughed till his eyes streamed with tears. "Oh dear, dear, dear. The innocence of the young makes a fool out of the wisdom of the ancients. I knew Manannan was keeping the staff safe. If I wasn't so distracted I would have realized all we had to do was ask. Well done, Chantel. Well done."

He stroked his staff and murmured something under his breath. The staff transformed into a large but normal-looking walking stick.

"Why are you disguising it?" said Chantel. "Aren't you going to use it, Myrddin? Please fix everything. Rescue Adam and magic everything else right."

Myrddin sobered up. "I will try, Little One. You have helped make us stronger. But we must keep my staff hidden for now. The Dark Being must not know you have retrieved it. As long as she thinks she can find our tools for herself she will not be in a rush to invade and destroy everything. If she realizes the tools are found, she will have nothing to lose and will confront us. We need time. Time to restring the necklace and waken the Lady. Time to rescue Adam and to fix whatever is wrong with Ava..." He stopped, seeing Chantel's happiness fade away. "Have faith, Little One. Keep the light in your heart. You have tipped the odds in our favor..."

With a clatter and a shout, Owen erupted into the holiday flat, closely followed by a harassed-looking Mr. Smythe.

Owen had cobwebs in his hair and smudges of dust on his face and clothes. He was waving an old wooden board in the air.

"Holly, Holly, you're gonna love this..." Owen brandished the board again. "I found the entrance to a secret passage in the cellar, and look what was inside..." Owen flashed the board at Mr. Smythe. "They're runes, aren't they?"

Mr. Smythe peered over his glasses. "They certainly are."

"I knew it," said Owen with great satisfaction. He thrust the board into Holly's hands. "You know what this is, don't you? It's that board you saw in your dream, the one with Breesha's name on it. It was in the secret passage..." He ran out of breath.

Owen rushed over to the sink in the galley kitchen, turned on the water and stuck first his mouth, then his face and head under the tap.

Holly laid the board on the table.

Owen re-joined them, shaking drips from his hair and wiping his mouth in his sleeve. "Fantastic, isn't it?"

"Owen! Go drip somewhere else." Holly held him at arm's length. "What makes you think this is the board from my dream? I know it looks old, but any one could scratch runes on an old piece of wood. It could be a joke. Or something for the Viking festival we've seen posters about, or..."

Owen bent down and shook his hair, wiped the drips from his face with his hands, and wiped his hands on the seat of his pants. "No, no, you don't get it. I asked Earth Magic to help me find the secret passage, and part of the cellar wall collapsed..."

Myrddin, Holly and Chantel gave a shout of laughter.

Mr. Smythe looked appalled.

"...and the board was by the entrance. I knew it was a magic board. Mr. Cubbon did too, but he won't tell. The runes were glowing in the dark. Mr. Cubbon distracted everyone so I could hide the board under my T-shirt before anyone else saw it. He helped me sneak it up here..."

Mr. Smythe moaned. "The landlord. What will the landlord say?"

"Don't worry about him," said Owen, laughing. "He's as pleased as punch. He says the passage will put him on the tourist map. He's already phoned the museum. There's a whole bunch of people down there now with torches and hard hats, exploring where it goes." His voice grew frustrated. "They won't let me go with them, in case it's not safe."

Holly wasn't listening. Gently she drew one finger over each rune, tracing them.

Chantel nudged Owen and pointed.

As Holly's finger passed, the runes shimmered for a moment, as though touched by sunlight.

"It *is* the magic board," whispered Holly.

Everyone pored over it.

"Runes are just scratches," said Chantel, disappointed.

"That's right. That's how they were invented," said Mr. Smythe. His voice was animated. Here was something he understood. "Runes developed from lines scratched on wood, to keep count of simple things: baskets of fish, or a number of days. Eventually they became more elaborate. People added cross lines so individual runes developed special meanings. An alphabet was developed, but because so few people could read it, it began to be used as a magical code."

Mr. Smythe took out his pencil and notebook and began scribbling.

"What does this say?" asked Chantel.

Mr. Smythe tore a page. "Here's the Futhark, work it out."

"Futhark?" chorused the cousins. They giggled.

Mr. Smythe laughed. "*F*, *U*, *Th*, *Ar*, *K*. The name comes from the sounds made by first five runes just like alphabet comes from the first two letters in our Greek alphabet: Alpha, Beta."

Holly chuckled. "Yup, we all knew that!"

They pored over the scrap of paper.

"It start's with a *K*."

"This letter's *U*."

"Two *L*'s are next."

"Is this *A* or *Y*?"

"*N*."

"*KULLYN*."

"Is it a name?" said Holly doubtfully.

"It's either Welsh or Manx," said Mr. Smythe. "I think it would be written *Cullyn* with a C in today's alphabet, and pronounced Hoolin." He paused and scratched his head. "I've come across it before, but I don't remember what it means. I'd have to look it up."

Myrddin clapped his hand on Mr. Smythe's shoulder. "Well, well, well. Holly was right, my friend. You have a role here."

"I...I do?"

"The museum is across the road. Instead of coming to Barrule with us, use your research skills to see if you can find reference to a rune board, or if the word *Cullyn* crops up in the history of Peel or Pheric's Isle."

Mr. Smythe looked like a condemned man with a reprieve. "I don't have to go through the dratted portal? I can stay here and research in the museum?"

Myrddin eyes twinkled. "You most certainly can." He

gathered the children together with a movement of his arms. "I will take the children, but we will meet back here for tea at five o'clock and have an early night..." He stopped and looked over to Mr. Smythe.

"SMYTHE, are you listening?" he roared.

Startled, Mr. Smythe dragged his attention away from the rune board. "Er...what was that...er...five for tea? Well, yes, of course." He turned back to the board.

Shaking his head, Myrddin marched down the corridor and opened the door into the street. Fog billowed in. He disappeared within its folds.

"Wait for us!" called Owen. "Bye, Mr. Smythe."

The three children rushed out, banging the door behind them.

Mr. Smythe was left at the table, gazing at the board. "Magic runes. How marvelous," he whispered. "What a day, what a day."

⁂

Adam surfaced gradually from his long heavy sleep, into a place of grayness. He had no idea if it was day or night, or even where he was.

His eyelids fluttered then half opened. He lay, thick with sleep, trying to think properly. "I was dreaming," he muttered. "Dreaming about flying like Ava."

Something tickled his chin.

He moved his hand from under his cheek. A feather, a soft piece of down, lay in his palm. "Ava?" he muttered. Memory stirred. He remembered flying, flying through mist, but as a boy on the end of a cloak, not as a bird. He stared at the feather again. It puzzled him. Where did it come from? It reminded him of a down-lined duck nest he'd once found. A wave of homesickness swept over him. He didn't know where he was, but it wasn't Earth. He'd give anything to be safely back there. He sniffed.

The feather flew up and tickled his nose. Adam gave a tiny grin and pulled it away. Could it be Ava's? He held it up in the grayness and it shimmered. He was still too sleepy to figure it out, but the words, "Keep the light in your heart," ran through his mind. Feeling comforted, he tucked the feather into his pocket and drifted off into another doze.

Mr. Cubbon emerged from the Castleview Inn, brushing cellar dust from his sweater. Puffing with exhaustion, he plumped down on the bench outside to catch his breath. Exciting things were happening. Magical things. Experiences he had not known since childhood were happening again. He was thrilled to be able to help the youngsters, and gleefully waiting to share some information with Owen. The museum people had discovered the passage ran to a smugglers cave on Pheric's Isle, but the raven had told him the real secret. All this was tiring though. He needed a little rest.

Mr. Cubbon leaned back, his chin drooped over his chest and his eyes closed.

Two Shades closed in on him.

"Magic, magic, I ssensse magic," hissed one Shade as it hovered behind the dozing fisherman.

"Not sso much, not sso much," sighed the other.

"Enough, enough. Sshall I meld? Sshall I? He knowss the nassty young humanss. Take uss to them he could, he could."

"They wouldn't ssensse uss, wouldn't ssensse uss?"

"They'd ssensse him, only him."

"Yess, yess. Sspy, sspy we will. Yess. Pleassed, the Dark One will be. Sso pleassed."

The first Shade pooled again at Mr. Cubbon's feet and melded into his body. The second Shade hovered nearby as his shadow.

⁂

A door banged shut. Mr. Cubbon woke with a jerk. He watched sleepily as Myrddin and the children made their way through the fog. They hadn't noticed him.

He rubbed his forehead. He'd been waiting for the children, but he couldn't remember why. He wasn't feeling well.

He eased himself up with difficulty. His body was shivering and shaking. He'd never felt so cold. He was chilled to the bone as though coming down with a flu. "Better get myself home," he muttered.

But it was hard to move. Hard to make himself walk up the hill to his cottage.

His feet wouldn't turn.

He felt compelled to follow the children.

The bang of a door made him jump again. He watched as

Mr. Smythe left the inn, crossed the road to the museum and disappeared inside. He felt no compulsion to follow him.

Mr. Cubbon rubbed his head again. Strange things were happening.

Everyone he knew was getting angry; that was why he'd left the cellar. People were raising voices and yelling for no real reason. Arguing about who was in charge and who should take credit for the discoveries.

Something was going on. Yes, that was why he had to follow the children! He couldn't remember what it was, but, they were up to something. A wave of anger swept over him. Those kids were up to something. He must find out what it was.

Mr. Cubbon walked through the fog like a robot, words pounding through his head, driving him on.

Follow the children.

Follow the children.

His mind rationalized his actions. Children were pesky critters. He needed to keep an eye on them, watch them. Those children were up to no good!

"Myrddin, please wait. You're walking too fast. We can't keep up with you," shouted Owen as Myrddin disappeared in the fog ahead.

"My apologies. Of course you can't. I was deep in thought." Myrddin paused and waved irritably at the billowing mist. "Manannan is overreacting with this cloak of mist, though I suspect he thinks something nasty might be following Equus."

"That's what I want to tell you," said Owen as he and the two girls caught up. He put his hand on Myrddin's arm and stood on tiptoe to whisper into Myrddin's ear. "Don't leave us behind. I think the 'something nasty' is following us."

They both swung around, peering into the fog on every side. Neither saw anything other than the vague shape of Mr. Cubbon in the distance.

Owen raised a hand, but Mr. Cubbon didn't respond.

Myrddin dropped his voice. "Explain."

"I feel eyes watching me, but there's never anyone there. It started when Mr. Cubbon and I were in the basement. It wasn't just me. Mr. Cubbon felt it too. He said something's been watching him ever since we arrived." Owen shivered. "It's really creepy. The feeling left when I went upstairs to the holiday flat." Owen glanced behind him. "It started again just now. As soon as I stepped outside the inn."

"Does anyone else sense this?"

Both girls shivered and nodded. "I thought I was imagining it because the mist was getting to me," murmured Holly.

"Me too," whispered Chantel.

"Then I will give you directions in mindspeak."

The children stood still and listened.

We will hasten to Fenella Beach, on the far side of the causeway. There we can talk without fear of being overheard. It is a place with its own magic and will offer us protection. It is the cove below the castle, Holly, so it is on your way as well as ours. Follow me.

Unnoticed, Mr. Cubbon also followed.

*If I remember rightly, the steps to the beach should be around here somewhere...*Muttering to himself in mind-speak, Myrddin cast about at the end of the causeway.

More fog blew in from the sea, and the children had difficulty seeing him again.

This way. Myrddin paused. He scattered something on the ground, muttered over it and began to vanish into the mist again.

Owen ran and grabbed the corner of Myrddin's cloak. He thrust out his other hand to grab Chantel. *Hang on too. Who knows where we're off to?*

Holly hung on to Chantel.

The children broke into a trot as they descended a boat ramp sloping toward the water.

Slow down, Myrddin. We'll fall! pleaded Chantel.

Apologies. Myrddin paused again. *I am driven by a feeling of urgency. I forget your stride is shorter than mine.* He helped them off the boat ramp, onto the sand.

Crossing Fenella Beach was terrifying.

The fog billowed in from the sea, hiding all but an arm's length in front of them. They had no sense of direction, or of their surroundings. They lurched and stumbled, sinking into wet sand or tripping over rocks or drifts of seaweed. Hidden waves hissed angrily on one side, and an invisible raven croaked a warning from above.

"Myrddin," whispered Holly. "This is horrible. How much farther? Can't we stop above the high tide line? Oops. Is it safe to talk?"

"We are safe. What is following will not enter the cove. I scattered stardust at the entrance, and the cove itself is still protected by Fenella's magic, though sadly, she may have faded away long ago."

A cliff loomed ahead, a scatter of rocks at its base. Myrddin chose one and seated himself.

"What the heck was watching me?" burst out Owen as he squatted beside Myrddin. "It felt horrid." He scrubbed the back of his neck with his hand.

"I fear some of the Dark Being's minions have found a way to slip into Man," Myrddin said. "She calls them Shades." He sighed. "They are the shadows of lives she destroyed on other planets. They couldn't find the courage to fade into the Mists of Time, choosing to serve her instead. Individually they have little power, but they can watch and spy. Like wraiths they emit negative feelings. Occasionally they can meld with someone, though usually not for long. When massed together, they become lethal.

"You all stepped into my stardust as you passed through the entrance to this beach. That will offer some protection, and here's a little more." Myrddin threw a handful of stardust over each child.

"A Shade will not be able to approach you to meld or to follow in your footsteps. However, I cannot prevent them spying from a distance, and their presence will affect your thoughts."

"Can you zap them, Myrddin?" Holly asked.

"You mean kill them?" Myrddin raised his eyebrows.

Holly looked shocked and shook her head.

"The Shades deserve your pity. They were living beings whose planet was 'zapped' as you say. I could help them face the Mists if they chose, but I would have to reveal my staff. The Dark Being must not know I have it yet."

"That's your real staff? It doesn't look like it," said Owen.

Myrddin waved his hand, and the staff gave Owen a glimpse of its full glory.

"Wow! Where did it come from? How did you get it back?" Owen could hardly contain himself.

Chantel grinned proudly.

Myrddin smiled. "The Myrddin is whole again, thanks to Chantel."

"Chantel?" Owen's eyes held real respect. "How on earth did you do that?"

Chantel grinned. "You used magic in the cellar. I used it in the bedroom. Manannan helped me."

Owen held out his palm. They exchanged high fives.

"Now children, tell me what Earth Magic is calling to you," said Myrddin.

"To rescue Adam, and there's white horses..."

"I must find Breesha's grave, but Adam..."

"We've gotta get Adam, but something's wrong with Ava..."

Everyone talked at once.

Myrddin banged his staff on a rock. "One at a time. One at a time."

Chantel tugged at his sleeve. "Rescue Adam. Please hurry and rescue Adam."

Holly linked her arm through Chantel's. "We might be able to help now that we can all mind read and mind-speak together. How far does our mindspeak go?" Holly hesitated. "Could we reach Adam?"

Myrddin looked thoughtful. "Interesting. Humans mindspeak a different way, on a different frequency, from Wise Ones.

"Equus, Ava and I had to learn to mindspeak with you. The Dark Being hears my usual mindspeak, but she might not catch yours. She won't expect you to have that skill."

"But what if she does? I don't want to talk to her." Holly sounded distressed.

Myrddin patted her shoulder. "Events have gone too far to worry about that. The Dark Being will be here soon. We will all face her. Follow your heart, Holly. It has served you well."

"Then I think we should try to contact Adam with mindspeak. And I think we should try it now."

The others nodded.

"I can help protect you," said Myrddin. "Which of you is going to speak?"

"Holly," said Chantel. "She's better at it than me." Her voice dropped. "And Adam will listen to her. He never believes me." Her lip trembled.

Holly gave her a sqeeze.

"Stand here, Holly." Myrddin used the base of his staff to draw a circle around her in the pebbly sand. He strengthened the circle with another scatter of stardust. "The thickening of the Mists of Time makes mindspeak harder. Do your best, Holly. Shout! We will all listen in."

Holly flashed a grin and closed her eyes.

Adam roused again. He still lay in grayness but his mind was a little clearer. He relaxed, letting the events of the previous night return to him.

He'd been hurt. His arms and shoulders had been sore because he'd hung on so long to Zorianna's cloak. His body stiffened as he remembered the journey through the mist and the tumble from the staff.

Adam shifted his shoulders and flexed his back muscles. He didn't hurt now. Why? Another memory surfaced: the vague image of the beautiful woman bending over him. That was it. He'd been rescued by the Lady.

Weak with relief, Adam relaxed under the comfort of the wrap she'd dropped over him. He couldn't believe how lucky he'd been. He'd actually entered that terrifying dark before the Lady had pulled him away. It was a pity he couldn't remember much about her. He'd been so terrified, exhausted and in such agony that everything was a blur. But she'd made the pain go away. Then he'd slept.

So where was he? In her house? In the stars?

His surroundings were still and gray. An amazing stillness, an eerie grayness. The stillness had been a welcome change when he arrived: a haven after the nightmare ride through the mist. But now it felt uneasy. This stillness around him wasn't a peaceful stillness. It was the stillness of emptiness. The Lady wasn't there. No one was.

He began to panic. Where the heck was he?

Adam...mindspeak...safe?

Fractured sentences floated into his mind.

He was dreaming? No...He was hearing Holly mindspeak!

He replied, giddy with relief.

Holly? Holly...I can hear you. I'm safe...But I don't know where I am. Everything's gray. The Lady rescued me. She is beautiful and kind, like you said.

He waited a long time for Holly's reply. Again the message was indistinct, like a bad telephone line.

Lady?...Myrddin rescue...Don't...

I can't hear you, Holly. I'm only getting a few words. Tell Myrddin I'm okay. I'm with the Lady. But I don't know where we are.

*Not...Not...*Holly's voice cut off.

No more words came through but feelings did. Strong feelings. Holly was scared, distressed and angry. Scared and distressed he understood, but why was she angry?

Adam mulled over the last message. *Not...Not...*Not what? But everything was such an effort. Trying to mindspeak had wiped him out again.

He wished things would make sense.

Maybe Holly was mad because he was with the Lady, not her. That must be it! Well, tough luck! Win some, lose some.

Adam gave a tiny yawn and drifted into yet another doze.

Holly's eyes were filled with horror. "Did you hear?"

"Yes," whispered Owen and Chantel. The same shock was mirrored in their faces.

"How could he mistake the Dark Being for the Lady?" ranted Holly. "How could he?"

"He said she was kind and beautiful." Chantel shuddered.

"She is most beautiful," rumbled Myrddin as he swept away the magic circle with his foot.

The children's eyes widened.

"The Dark can be as beautiful as the Light."

The children were silent.

"Holly, you did well warning Adam," said Myrddin.

"But he didn't understand. He thinks she's the Lady. What if he helps her?" Holly was shaking.

Myrddin touched Holly's shoulder. "It is a shock, but trust both in Adam and Old Magic. This has happened for a reason."

Holly nodded and breathed deeply, allowing Myrddin's magical strength to flow through her.

"Time presses. I must join Manannan, Ava and Equus now. Rest assured I will share this new development with them, and we will find a way to rescue Adam. You have done your utmost to warn him. You must put it behind you, Holly, for now you have other tasks."

Holly took several more steadying breaths and met Myrddin's eyes. "I'm fine. It was just a shock."

Myrddin squeezed her shoulder gently and removed his hand. "Follow your heart and find Breesha's grave, Holly. Listen to the Earth Magic. Have faith that Adam will also listen to what's in his heart."

He pointed with his staff to some well-concealed steps cut into the rock cliff behind them. "Go. These steps lead to the castle gate. Taking them will outwit the Shade."

"Are you going to meet Ava and Equus?" Owen asked.

Myrddin nodded. "Of course. Do you wish to accompany me?"

Owen hesitated. "Yes and no. I want to help Ava and I want to rescue Adam, but I don't have those powers, and we're running out of time."

"Go on, boy."

"I've been thinking about the castle."

"Yes?"

Holly swung around from examining the steep steps up the cliff. She looked eagerly at Owen.

"We're heading for a big bust-up with the Dark Being, aren't we?" Owen asked Myrddin.

Myrddin nodded.

"Then the castle is the best place for it. You said it was the most magical place on Gaia."

"I did."

"So I should explore it. Find places to hide and to fight. None of us knows the castle. Scoping it out would give us a better chance."

"Ahh. The young warrior wishes to hone his skills. The confrontation with the Dark may not be a fight of arms, Owen."

"I know, I know. But when we were with the dragon in the first adventure and with Zorianna in the Tor, it wasn't just magic that worked, it was us being human and doing things they didn't expect. If I explore the castle, I might be able to come up with some unexpected things that would help."

Myrddin laughed. "You are correct, young warrior. Your tactics are sound. Go to the castle with Holly, and may you find many unexpected things."

"Brilliant, Owen," said Holly. "I'd love some company. These steps look pretty creepy in the fog."

"What about me?" Chantel's voice was wistful.

Myrddin smiled. "You are not forgotten, Chantel. Come, it is time for you to call the Cabbyl Ushtey."

Chantel's voice was a squeak. "Call who?"

"The Cabbyl Ushtey, the white horses you saw in the waves. They will appear at your request, for you are the Magic Child called by Equus. Use mindspeak, though there is no one around to see or overhear."

"You are wrong, Myrddin. I hear."

Myrddin swung around, his face full of joy. "Fenella, you remain! So few on Gaia remember Old Magic. I didn't dare hope."

A woman in white hovered beside them. She was as transparent as a ghost. "I am always here, until there is no one left who remembers me. One human sees me still. His visits keep me from fading away into the mist."

"Is that Mr. Cubbon? He was a Magic Child once," said Chantel softly.

"That is his name. He is lonely. He comes to talk with me and the ravens. Now you see me, Myrddin, and I gain more strength."

"Us too. We can see and speak to you," Owen pointed out.

The woman laughed. "I grow stronger by the second."

Though still flimsy, she did seem more substantial.

"Call not for the Cabbyl Ushtey. It is hard for them to transform and step on land. Their strength, like mine, is weak. So few see them."

Chantel jabbed Owen. "Told ya," she whispered.

He grinned and gave her a mock bow.

"They will be needed later, for I sense a great Darkness approaching," continued Fenella. "The child should visit them in their own realm." She drifted toward the water's edge. "Friends may request my magic."

"Thank you, Fenella." Myrddin bowed. "Make your request, Child."

Chantel stepped before Fenella. She stood with her hands clasped behind her back, looking very young and very sincere.

"Er...Please can you help me visit the Cabb...Cabbyl Ushtey?"

She looked across at Myrddin to see if she had got the name right. He nodded and encouraged her with a wave of his hand.

"We will need their help, so I should talk to them."

Fenella cupped her hand and called softly over the water.

"Manannan Beg Mac y Lair,
Mie goll magh as ny share goll stiagh,
Manannan Beg Mac y Leir,
Give safe journey out and a better journey home."

A small round boat floated out of the mist and bobbed to their feet.

"Wow, a coracle!" said Owen. "One of the earliest boats ever made." He ran over and grabbed, pulling it into the shallows. It was as light as a feather.

The boat was made of skins stretched tightly across

a circular framework of split willow. A wooden paddle lay on the bottom.

"Fear not the Cabbyl Ushtey," said Fenella. "They will honor you and gain strength from your visit. Tell them Fenella says neither the Mists of Time nor Manannan's cloak will hold the Dark One at bay, and that the Wise Ones have come to stand with Manannan." She motioned Chantel to the boat.

"Fear not the coracle. It knows its way. Fear not the sea. It is the Cabbyl Ushteys' realm and part of the Sleeper's magic."

"Can I show Chantel how the coracle works?" Without waiting for an answer, Owen hopped inside the tiny craft with one leg and pushed off from the beach with the other. He sat crosslegged on the bottom and wielded the paddle. "Wheee!" The boat spun around like a top.

"Owen," thundered Myrddin, "show a little more respect."

Owen grinned, but brought the coracle under control. He bobbed in and out of the mist, just beyond the breaking waves.

"Sorry," he called. "But I've always wanted a coracle. I tried to make one when I was a little kid. It sank."

"OWEN," roared Myrddin.

Owen dug in the paddle and shot back to the beach on the crest of the next wave. He hopped out and held the boat steady for Chantel. "Did you get the idea? It's real easy?"

Chantel laughed and slapped his hand away from the side of the craft. "This is my magic. You find your own."

Myrddin prodded her with his staff. "Step in, step in."

Chantel scrambled inside. Ignoring the paddle, she knelt, clutching the rim of the tiny craft with her hands.

"Farewell. Let light and truth keep fear at bay as you enter the realm of the Cabbyl Ushtey." Fenella made a graceful pushing motion with her hands.

The coracle swooshed out to sea with Chantel's upright body parting the mist, leaving it billowing and swirling behind her.

Holly sighed. "She looks awfully small. Will she be all right, Myrddin?"

"She'll be splendid," said Myrddin softly as he watched the coracle disappear. "Chantel has a special magic, the magic of innocence." He turned away from the waves. "As for you, Holly. Go to the castle and take that pesky brother with you." He poked Owen in the small of his back. "Be gone, boy. It is time to devise irritations for the Dark Being, not for me."

Suppressing grins, Holly and Owen scrambled up the flight of rocky stairs and disappeared in the fog.

"My thanks, Fenella. May you never fade," said Myrddin with a bow. He stamped his staff on the ground and swirled his cloak.

"Manannan Beg Mac y Leir, I pray you a portal," he shouted and vanished in a flash of light.

Chantel leaned forward eagerly as her craft cut through the gray waves, bobbing and tilting this way and that. The water hissed and slapped beneath her, but she trusted the magic, laughing as the wind whipped her hair. She tasted salt spray on her lips. She didn't try to paddle. She held the sides and watched for white horses.

At first she saw only glimpses. From the corner of her eye she'd spot a flowing mane, the flick of a white tail. Each time she turned, they vanished.

Just once, a beautiful white head with silver eyes rose beside her and stared deep into her eyes, before dissolving back into the foam crest of a passing wave.

Chantel sang to Cabbyl Ushtey in mindspeak, the way she sang to the ponies she rode. *Oh you beauties, don't be scared, I'll never hurt you. I'm a friend of Equus. Please can I meet with you? We need your help.*

She checked each passing wave for another glimpse of the magical beasts.

With a shower of white spray, the coracle was surrounded. Six Cabbyl Ushtey closed in, three on each side.

The white horses pressed closer and closer, crowding the tiny boat with their shoulders. As the frame began to bend, they dove.

Down went the coracle and Chantel, slicing through the water like a turtle. Chantel's red curls streamed behind her. Bubbles streamed past her, and magically, she could breathe! Smiling, she stretched out her arms and clutched handfuls of the nearest flowing manes.

The Cabbyl Ushtey tossed their heads and guided her coracle deep into the watery depths of their realm.

⁂

Mr. Cubbon came to a sudden stop at the top of the boat

ramp that dropped down to Fenella Beach. He couldn't move forward. An invisible barrier blocked his way.

A hot wave of anger consumed him. This was his beach. How could something stop him going down? It must be those kids. He knew they were up to something. How dare they magic him out! Somehow he must discover what they were up to.

He tried to force his body forward again, but a wave of nausea and dizziness shook him. He swayed and shivered. Dratted flu. Better sit. He tottered over the causeway to a bench by the castle and sank down, lowering his head to his hands in an attempt to stop it spinning.

※※※

Repulsed by the scattering of stardust at the entrance to Fenella's Beach, the Shade that had melded with Mr. Cubbon oozed from his body, and the Shade that shadowed him detached.

Both took to the sky, circling high overhead.

Though they could sense the human children below, they could see nothing through the fog.

Earth Magic and Old Magic tingled, not only from the cove, but also from the castle rising on top of the cliffs.

One Shade called out, a soundless cry that only other Shades heard. "Come, come, come. Here iss magic, much, much magic. Come ssee, ssee, ssee."

The Shades circling Gaia flowed back to join them. Like black shadows, they gathered around Pheric's Isle, but Manannan's magical web repulsed them. They hovered like vultures above it.

Watching. Waiting.

The first two Shades also watched the old man slumped below. His body might be needed again.

<hr>

Adam slid into wakefulness again. This time it felt different. His mind was clear and focused, his memory complete. The feeling of exhaustion was gone. Though he lay surrounded with grayness he felt filled with light.

Adam stretched and yawned, then considered his situation.

He had no way of knowing where he was. That was bad.

He was safe and comfortable and had Ava's feather. That was good.

The Lady had rescued him. That was wonderful.

But she had disappeared. Hmm, a little worrying.

He cleared his throat and called out, "Lady? Lady? Is anyone here?"

She appeared instantly, clapping her hands and laughing in delight. "You are awake at last, courageous child. Can you stand?" She drew Adam to his feet. "Come. Refresh yourself at my table. I am the Lady Doona, but please don't stand on ceremony. You may call me Doona." She tossed her head, running one hand through the shining black curls. "Obviously it means 'dark maiden.'" She chuckled.

Adam answered her with a grin. "I get called 'Red' sometimes."

"Ahh, you and I have much to discuss. Come come."

They entered a dimly lit room where Doona showed

Adam to a bench piled high with silk cushions. At least twenty dishes of delicious-looking finger foods and sweet-meats were set on the low table before it.

"I feel like a character in *The Arabian Knights*," Adam said awkwardly.

Doona's chuckle bubbled around him. She pressed a fragrant goblet of some strange juice into his hand.

Adam drained it, hunger and thirst overcoming him for a moment.

"Sit and eat," said Doona, patting the cushions. "Tell me all about yourself and how I came to find you falling through the mist."

Adam opened his mouth to speak, but something about the opulence of the room put him off. It made him feel uncomfortable as though he was in the middle of a stage set. He played for time by eating a chocolate from the nearest dish. His mind buzzed. "I don't know where to start," he mumbled.

"First, who are you?"

"I'm Adam Maxwell, from Canada." The floodgates opened. Adam told about himself and Chantel and their troubled parents. "They sent us away, to England, to stay with our cousins," Adam said with a catch in his throat. "And that was when the magic started," he finished.

A beringed hand patted his knee. "Aah, yes. Tell me about the magic and meeting the Wise Ones," Doona said gently. "Aeons have passed since I last saw them."

Adam nodded. He ate another chocolate and drank from a fresh goblet. "The Wise Ones have missed you. They always call you the Lady. We have been waiting for ages, hoping you would come to help us. See, there are just the four of us. Four Magic Children to help you four Wise Ones find your Tools. Holly's dying to meet you." He grinned. "She'll be mad I met you first, because it's her turn to help.

"Chantel helped Equus regain his talisman. Owen uncovered Ava's circlet. Then Ava and Equus went off to fix the Land Beyond Morning while I helped Myrddin." He stopped, distressed. "And I did it! I found Myrddin's staff. But Zorianna, the Dark Being's emissary, snatched it away. I...I grabbed her cloak...and it was awful." Adam managed to control his voice, but his body trembled. "I was swept into the Mists and...and...I fell...and was nearly sucked into the Dark Being's realm." He looked up and met the beautiful eyes that stared down at him. "Thank goodness you rescued me," he finished simply.

Doona stood up and paced. "Things have become more complicated than I imagined," she said.

Adam nodded. "Everyone's hoping you'll wake up and come to help." A look of puzzlement crossed his face. "They thought you were sleeping."

"Ahh," Doona came and sat beside Adam. She took both his hands in hers and looked deep into his eyes.

"I have to tell you something that's been kept from you. Something that will change everything. You must listen very carefully."

"Okay," said Adam. He shifted on the cushions.

"There are five Wise Ones, not four. I am not the sleeping Lady..."

Adam pulled his hands away and jumped to his feet.

"Adam, panic not. I am the Lady Doona, the fifth Wise One. The Lady's sister."

Adam's face cleared. "You are?"

Doona nodded and patted the cushions once more. "Come back, child. Let me tell you about my family.

"Equus and Ava were too embarrassed, too loyal, to tell you the whole story. For despite our magical powers, my family, like yours, had a terrible fight that split us apart."

Doona's eyes pooled with tears. "I was the young one sent away. I was abandoned. I nearly died."

She dashed at the tears with one hand and held out the other to Adam.

He squeezed it tightly. "Why? What was the fight about?"

"My necklace."

Adam gasped. "It's yours?"

Doona nodded sadly. "It was taken from me by force, and I was cast out. But the necklace will help no one unless I wear it. That is why the Lady ignores your calls."

"Bu–but what about the other Wise Ones? They must know."

"They know, but were embarrassed to tell you the whole story—Wise Ones fighting like humans. What would you think? Maybe you would refuse to help them.

"Equus, Ava and Myrddin are trying to retrieve the necklace peacefully. Once all three of them have their Tools, the Lady will have to surrender. Then they will return the necklace quietly to me, and the Dark Being will be no more."

Confused, Adam sagged back into the cushions. A massive headache began to pound. The combination of rich food, heady drink and so much startling information was overloading him.

Doona placed a gentle hand on his forehead.

The pain eased, but her touch made his eyelids droop.

"I am sorry," Doona murmured. "This burden is heavy. Rest again, child. We will talk later. Will you help me?"

Adam nodded as his heavy eyelids shut. He curled gratefully among the silken pillows as Doona drifted away.

He knew he needed time. Time to think this through, to examine everything he'd heard.

Something wasn't right.

He thrust his hand in his pocket to touch Ava's feather. If only there was light!

Adam's doze was brief but refreshing, but he didn't sit up immediately. He lay still. His mind buzzed, sifted around, struggled to piece together unconnected bits of information.

He liked Doona, but he sensed she hadn't told him everything.

The Wise Ones obviously hadn't either.

And something had stopped him telling Doona everything. He hadn't told her about hearing Holly's mindspeak. Why? Was it because Holly's words contained a missing piece of information he needed?

Adam thought back to Holly's mindspeak, and the feeling of anger, shock and another emotion that had come with it.

What was the other emotion that had pervaded Holly's words?

FEAR!

The word slipped into his mind as clearly as if it had been shouted aloud.

Holly was terrified. Why?

Adam went through his memory of the mindspeak conversation word by word. The wave of fear from Holly wasn't there at the beginning. It came when he mentioned the Lady.

There had been a pause. Holly had said *Not... Not...* accompanied by the wave of fear.

Adam's stomach lurched as his mind completed Holly's fractured mindspeak—*Not the Lady. Not the Lady.*

But why was that frightening? Doona had admitted she wasn't the Lady. She was the Lady's sister.

The answer whispered in the back of his mind. He tried to ignore the idea. It would not be ignored.

Fear washed over Adam, and he knew his answer was right. His whole being knew it.

Lady Doona was the Dark Being!

That explained her story, his unease, Holly's fear, everything.

Adam curled into a ball.

He was Adam the idiot, Adam the useless. He'd assumed Doona was good because she was kind and beautiful. But she was the Dark Being. Deep in his subconscious, he'd always known but had not dared admit it. But the clarity of his thoughts would no longer let him believe a lie.

The hair on the back of his neck prickled.

Doona was there. He could sense her. The Dark Being had entered the room again and was staring down at him.

Adam's mind raced. There was only one course of action he could take.

In order to survive, he must act a part. Act as he had never acted before. What he had to do next required an Oscar performance for Best Actor. He must convince the Dark Being that he was on her side.

Adam shuddered, but turned it into a stretch.

He peeped under his lashes.

The Dark Being was turning away, the remains of a smile hovering on her lips.

Adam caught his breath. She was even more beautiful than he remembered. How could she be evil?

He watched as she stretched out one hand and pulled a hole in the grayness surrounding them. She leaned forward and stared down at something far below.

Adam could only see the side of her face, but there was no mistaking the change of expression that crossed it. Her features were contorted into a snarl of hatred.

Adam yawned loudly and sat up.

The Dark Being turned, all smiles again.

"How delightful! You are rested again, Adam, the courageous?" She clapped her hands and a shadow appeared. It drifted toward Adam and placed a fresh tray containing another goblet and some cake-like food beside him, then drifted back into the grayness.

Adam controlled another shudder. "Hi, Doona," he said, and returned a brilliant smile.

CHAPTER EIGHT

THE PAGAN LADY

AARCK, AARCK.

The raven's cry floated through Manannan's cloak of mist.

It startled Owen. He missed his footing on the narrow cliff steps and stumbled forward, sprawling on hands and knees. One leg slipped over the drop. Shaken, Owen drew it back and paused for a moment, huddling against the rock face. He drew his knee up to his chin and rubbed the shin, while trying to regain his nerve. He hated heights. "If we survive this so-called path without killing ourselves it will be a miracle," he muttered. "Myrddin's got rocks in his head sending us up here."

Holly saved her breath and concentrated on the uneven steps. She scrambled the last few meters on hands and feet, and stood panting on the cliff top, looking with relief at the narrow fringe of grass that ran between the castle walls and the cliff edge. "We've made it," she said. "Come on." She held her hand over the edge to Owen. He stretched and grabbed. She heaved.

Owen emerged and rolled on his back on the grass to recover.

"That was some climb," he said when he could breath again. He stood and stared down into the mist, venting his feeling by kicking a loose stone over the edge. It seemed ages before it clattered on the hidden beach below. Owen grinned wryly. "At least the fog concealed the drop."

AARCK, AARCK.

The raven swooped overhead and flew to the top of the gatehouse.

"Follow that bird," said Holly.

Owen raised a cupped hand to his mouth. "Aarck, Aarck...We're coming. We're coming," he croaked.

"Shhh," said Holly. "Don't alert the Shades."

Quaking in his shoes, Adam stood before the Dark Being. He wished he hadn't taken this route, but it was too late now. He'd convinced Doona that he was her man.

She summoned a Shadow. It appeared obediently and drifted to his side.

The Dark Being smiled down at them both. "You please me, Adam, the courageous. You will be a fine helper, so I send you back to Gaia with a tool. I hear that Gaia possesses only simple magic. My Shades have a skill humans do not. They can send mind messages a great distance."

Adam's eyes flickered. He dropped them quickly.

"As I need information, and you cannot mindspeak, I attach this Shade to you. To humans it will look like your shadow. It will not interfere with your actions in any way. Its only job is to listen and report back to me."

"It will tell you everything I say?" asked Adam. His voice wobbled.

"Is that a problem?" The Dark Being's question had a steely edge.

"Not really," said Adam. "But I might have to play along to get Owen and Holly on my side." He gave a small grin. "You won't get mad, will you?"

The Dark Being brushed aside his concern. "Of course not. The Shade will not repeat conversations, just content. It knows what information I need."

"Will it...will it make me do things I don't want to do?"

"No." The Dark being chuckled. "Don't be fearful, Adam, the courageous. I give you a tool. I have forbidden the Shade to meld with you. It will not control you. You are free to help me in your own way."

Adam tried not to shudder. "Thank you," he managed.

"Adam, you understand who I am and how badly I've been treated?"

Adam forced himself to meet her eyes again. "Yes, of course, Doona."

"Then I have a gift as well as a tool for you. I always reward my helpers. Give me your hand."

Adam lifted his left hand.

Doona's touch was cool as she slipped onto his finger a thin gold ring with a tiny black stone sunk into the band.

He spread his fingers as if he were admiring it. "Real gold, wow, thank you." He forced a smile through tight lips.

Doona laughed and touched his cheek. Her other hand touched the grayness of the Shade. Her eyes closed and reopened. "It is done."

Adam had felt nothing, but the Shade was no longer beside him. He looked down. A darker patch lay in the grayness at his feet. He took a few steps. It followed. Not quite a real shadow, but not strange enough that anyone would notice.

He felt nausea rising, but he swallowed and forced himself to smile again. "You're very clever," he said.

───

The Shades on Gaia were on high alert. They circled above the magic web that protected Pheric's Isle, glaring at Manannan's gulls that slipped back and forth at will.

The Shades studied the gulls' movements, hoping to unlock their magic. They had tried to meld with the birds, but the gulls could sense them and were too wily to be caught.

Angrily the Shades stared down through drifts of mist.

"Children, children, children approaching. Nassty human children," hissed one.

"I ssensse magic, sso much magic," said another.

"Tell the Dark One, we musst, we musst," said the third Shade.

Their heads nodding and bobbing in agreement, they gathered together.

"Sslide, sslide, sslide into one.

Thicken the darkness.

Sstrengthen the bondss."

Their shadows merged into one shadow, and a strong mind message fought its way through the Mists of Time and sped to the Dark Being.

***

"There's Mr. Cubbon. What's wrong with him?" Owen ran to the bench seat by the castle gatehouse and placed his hand on the shoulder of the slumped fisherman. "Are you all right, sir?"

Mr. Cubbon raised his head from his hands, a surprised look on his face. He smiled up at the boy and nodded.

"Aye, aye. I'm fine now. Thought I had a touch of the flu. Must have walked it off." He stood up and beamed at Holly and Owen. "Going to explore the castle are yer?"

The children nodded, their eyes serious.

The old man leaned forward. "I'd be careful if I were you. Strange things lurk on Pheric's Isle," he whispered. "Keep wits about you. Avoid the Moddy Dhoo and listen to the raven."

"We will," Holly said. She flashed him a smile and turned to go.

Mr. Cubbon pulled Owen aside. "I've news," he hissed.

Owen cocked his head as Mr. Cubbon bent to his ear.

"The secret passage...I know where it goes."

Owen's eyes sparkled. He caught his breath.

Mr. Cubbon's voice dropped even lower. "Under the estuary to a cave on Pheric's Isle. But there's a hidden part. Comes up in the round tower. The raven told me. Watch yer step."

"Wow! Thanks, Mr. Cubbon," Owen whispered. He patted the old man's arm and followed Holly up the wide worn sandstone stairs through the gatehouse to the ticket booth.

Myrddin materialized on Barrule's summit within the horsehoe wall of rocks.

The mountain fell steeply away on all sides, but there was no view. Everything below was blanketed with clouds. Only Barrule's bleak peak poked through, along with several other mountains to the north.

The sun shone, but the air was cold. Myrddin's hair and cloak streamed and flapped as a strong gust of wind buffeted him. He staggered for a moment and stumbled on a patch of loose scree.

He spotted Manannan and Equus lower down the slope, within the shelter of one of the great ditches.

Manannan was watching for him and raised an arm in greeting. His upturned face reflected obvious relief at Myrddin's arrival.

Myrddin raised his staff and strode down to join them.

The children prevailed. You are whole again. Equus's mindspeak met him, filled with gladness.

I have my staff. I am whole again. Myrddin's answer was equally heartfelt. *But what has happened to Ava?*

She challenged the vortex to let a speck of light into the Dark Being's presence. The edge of the Dark touched her. It consumes her. She's on my back. She needs pure light. Manannan has tried to heal her within a stone circle here on Mann. The light was not strong enough.

Myrddin jumped into the ditch and bowed low to Manannan.

"Greetings, my friend. Forgive our invasion of your island and our bringing of the Darkness."

"The Darkness came of its own accord," countered Manannan, bowing equally low. "You bring Light and are thrice welcome. How may I help you further?"

Myrddin gestured to Ava. "We need magic stronger than Earth Magic. Ava is helpless until she bathes in light streaming directly from the Place Beyond Morning. We need an Old Magic circle that is also protected and fortified."

"Then you must enter the magic realm in my care. We will reactivate the top of what the humans call the 'Round Tower' on Pheric's Isle. Though unused for aeons, the Tower is the heart of Gaia's magic, a raised and fortified circle forming a beacon to the stars. It is sheltered by an enchanted castle, encircled by the realm of water. Entities of earth support it, and it is protected from above by an invisible web of magic."

"Then grant us leave to enter your magic realm, Manannan."

"Leave is granted, Myrddin," replied Manannan

formally. "But know the beacon will be seen throughout the universe."

"There is no other way to heal Ava."

"So be it." Manannan blew. A great wind swirled, lifted all four beings and swept them away.

Their message dispatched to the Dark Being, the Shades hovered again above the protective web over Pheric's Isle.

One cried out in frustration. "Ssee insside, insside. The children come. Ssee, ssee!"

The blowing mist only allowed short glimpses of Holly and Owen in the castle ruins.

"Sspy, sspy by melding we will," chanted two Shades and swooped down again toward the unsuspecting Mr. Cubbon as he made his way back across the causeway.

"Sstoronger, sstronger. Together thiss time, meld, meld, meld," the Shades encouraged each other. They landed on the old fisherman's back, a dark stain on his sweater that quickly faded.

Mr. Cubbon staggered, then straightened. He turned and marched back to Pheric's Isle, his face once again contorted with rage.

"You're a keen pair of visitors," said the ticket woman, laughing as she took the castle entrance fee from Holly and Owen. "Fancy sightseeing in this fog. We didn't expect a soul this afternoon. It will be just you, me and the archaeologists."

"Archaeologists?" Holly echoed.

The woman nodded. "They're excavating a grave on the far side of the ruined cathedral. It's so exciting. I keep sneaking out to look. They've found bones and some grave goods. Ask them to show you the beautiful beads."

Holly gave a tiny gasp.

"You can't miss the dig, even in the mist," continued the woman. She thrust a map of the castle at Holly. "You're here, see?" She pointed with her finger to the map, then looked up and gestured with her arm. "Just bear to the right at the top of the steps and follow the walk. You'll get there."

"Er, could I have a map too, please?" asked Owen. "Just in case we get separated."

"Of course," said the woman. She passed one over.

"Who needs a map?" Holly whispered as they walked toward the steps.

The raven had fluttered down and was stepping deliberately before them, occasionally turning its black head to check that they were following.

Holly and Owen made their way through a strange and eerie world.

The castle walls loomed high, enclosing them, screening them from the outside. The mist restricted vision and made the ruins into an endless maze.

Owen nudged Holly as they passed a battery of ancient cannons pointing through narrow slits, but the raven didn't pause. It led them through arches opening onto roofless rooms, past billows of mist gathering in hollows formed by caved-in buildings, up steps at the base of crumbling walls and over a lawn to a grassy rise.

The mist deadened sound.

No wind reached them, no voices, no hissing of waves or cries from the gulls. It was as though the world held its breath.

Holly's shoes squeaked on the damp grass.

"Shhh," hissed Owen, then wondered why.

Ahead, shadowy figures stirred in the mist, and a sudden burst of laughter broke the spell. The raven soared to a perch on the nearest wall.

The children leaned over a rope barrier and looked down. Owen felt Holly stiffen. Several people squatted around a shallow excavation. Rock slabs, marked with fluttering tabs were stacked on one side of the dig. A heap of white quartz stones lay on the other. Between them lay the outline of a rocky grave containing the remains of a small, fragile skeleton.

Holly began to tremble. "Breesha," she murmured. A tear welled up and trickled unnoticed down her cheek. Whatever she'd imagined in finding the grave, it wasn't this. Earth Magic was full of surprises.

Owen watched with interest as a young woman with a soft brush cleaned a half buried leg bone.

A man scraped dirt, a bit at a time, from between an arm bone and a rib. He placed the dirt in a bucket.

A second man paced around taking close-up photos.

An older woman sifted the buckets of soil painstakingly, stopping to pick out a small object with a pair of tweezers. "Found another bead," she sang out. She held it up between the tweezers' tips, and gently blew dust away. "Blue glass, by the looks of things."

Holly reached out to Owen, grabbed his hand and squeezed hard.

Owen squeezed back.

A man appeared. The woman dropped the bead into his palm. He disappeared into a makeshift hut beyond the dig.

"Hello, we've got visitors." The woman brushing the leg bone had stopped to stretch. She waved. "Come to admire the Pagan Lady?" she asked.

Holly gulped and nodded, glad the mist obscured her teary eyes.

"Beautiful, isn't she?" The woman patted the leg bone. "We think she must have been someone really important. She's nearly a thousand years old and was buried with some amazing grave goods. It you walk around to the hut, Mitch will give you a peek at the necklace she was wearing. It's wonderful. We've found sixty-nine beads and are still finding more."

Shaken and speechless, the two children made their way beyond the grave to the hut.

* * *

Mr. Cubbon clambered up the steps to the gatehouse and bullied his way into the castle, dismissing the ticket person with a brusque, "Don't be silly, woman. Why should I pay for a tour around the castle? I only need to find them dratted kids."

Taken aback, the woman bridled. "No need to be rude, Mr. Cubbon. They're doing no harm. They went to the dig."

Mr. Cubbon pushed past her.

Breesha's beads lay in a tray on a makeshift table. A bright lamp shone down on them.

The man called Mitch hovered over them, the newly discovered bead between his finger and thumb. With a swift movement, his hand darted down and placed the blue glass between two like-sized beads, one red, one amber.

Holly gave a tiny sigh and an almost invisible shake of her head.

"Isn't this an incredible find?" The man turned to the children, bubbling with enthusiasm. "We think this beautiful necklace means our grave belongs to a woman of some stature. The wife of a chief. Or maybe the Manx wife of a Viking explorer who brought beads back to her from each trip."

He strode to the doorway of the hut and pointed beyond the walls, to where the sea would be seen if the mist lifted. "Imagine the scene: The explorer sails away on a Viking longboat and is gone for months, maybe years. Suddenly his sails are spotted. The women and children run down to the shore to meet him and his crew." Mitch took Holly's arm and led her back to the table. He picked up a large amber disk. "The explorer sweeps the woman into his arms and presses into her palm a fabulous bead from a strange new land." He pressed the disk into Holly's hand. "Trip by trip, the necklace grows longer and more spectacular. Trip by trip, her status grows." He grinned down at the children.

Holly held the amber and stared up at him. Her fingers itched and tingled with magic. The black bead in her pocket grew hot against her leg. "What if she was the visitor and turned up on the island with the beads already around her neck, and everyone thought it was a magical necklace?" she said seriously.

Mitch laughed and retrieved the disk. "Good thinking, but unlikely. Women didn't explore. Much more likely to be my scenario." He paused. "People might attribute magical powers to the unusual beads though...interesting idea." He laughed and replaced the disk on the tray. The children's eyes followed it.

"We'll never know. Archaeology is based on facts. The facts are that we have found a non-Christian woman—a pagan lady—buried with unusual care and a variety of grave goods, including the remains of this fabulous necklace. The rest is just my imagination." He looked down at the beads. "We're even guessing the order the beads were strung in. Fascinating, isn't it?" He smiled at the children.

The jet bead in Holly's pocket irritated and itched. Holly tried not to touch it, but she felt as though the bump was so obvious the man must be able to see it. Her mind raced. How could they distract him and drop the bead into the tray.

A woman's voice called out. "Found another bead."

Mitch rushed out of the hut.

Swiftly Holly pulled the black bead from her pocket and held it over the tray.

A voice she knew growled. "You're stealing! You rotten kids, I knew something were up. You're pinching beads!"

Shocked, Holly swung round.

Mr. Cubbon stood in the doorway, his face no longer friendly but contorted with hatred. He pointed an accusing finger. A wave of malevolence, so strong it was almost physical, swept over them.

Dropping the bead in the tray, Holly pushed past the old man and fled into the mist.

Owen followed.

"Stop 'em. They're stealing beads," shouted Mr. Cubbon.

A gigantic hue and cry rose from the dig as the workers dropped tools and gave chase.

Most of the Shades were riveted, watching events unfold in the castle below. But one still watched the gulls slipping so easily back and forth through the magical mesh.

Time and time again it tried to meld with a gull. Time and time again it failed. At last its careful observation paid off.

"Ssee, ssee," the Shade cried. "The birds eat fissh. Watch, watch." It left the other Shades to slide into the sea where gulls dove through the waves and feasted on a school of herring.

"Fissh, fissh, meld with the fissh," called the Shade. It melded with the nearest herring.

A greedy gull gulped. The herring vanished.

The bird soared up, passed through the web of magic and landed on a wall on Pheric's Isle.

"Ssee, ssee, ssee," squawked the gull. "Copy me, copy me, copy me!"

With soundless cries of triumph, the Shades descended to the surface of the sea and melded with fish.

Leaping and flashing through the waves, the herring soon attracted the attention of more gulls who swooped down and swallowed them.

The possessed gulls soared through the magical web. Their shrieks of triumph rang through the air.

"Ssearch for the children! Ssearch for the children! Ssearch for the children!"

***

Holly fled through the ruins. Owen followed.

They scrambled over a low wall and tumbled down an unexpected slope on the far side.

Swiftly finding her feet, Holly raced on. Owen stuck to her heels: up mounds, between walls, down passageways, through arches.

Behind them feet pounded and voices shouted. Gulls screamed and swooped over their heads.

It was the mist that saved them.

Holly dove headfirst into a mist-filled hollow and rolled into a hidden corner. She sat gasping for breath.

Owen followed and hunkered down beside her.

"Why run?" he panted. "You'd done nothing wrong."

"I couldn't stand the hate, and I was holding the black bead. Try explaining that!" Holly gasped.

"Still got it?" asked Owen.

Holly shook her head. "I dropped it in the tray with the others." Her eyes filled with tears. "What are we going to do?

No one will let me near the beads now. I've failed Breesha and messed everything up. The beads are in the wrong order, Owen. They need sorting as well as restringing."

Owen clapped his hand gently over her mouth and jerked his head.

Voices floated through the mist.

"This is hopeless. They could be anywhere in the castle."

"Why waste time looking? There's only one entrance and exit. Sooner or later they're going to use it."

"You're right. Stupid kids."

"Did they pinch anything?"

"Don't know yet. Mitch is counting the beads." The voices faded away.

Owen grinned. "I'd like to be a fly on the wall when they realize there's an extra," he whispered. "And as for one entrance, they've got that wrong too."

"How come?"

"Mr. Cubbon told me. The secret passage from Castleview Inn leads to the Round Tower."

"Mr. Cubbon thinks I'm a thief. He hates us," said Holly, a catch in her voice.

Owen frowned. "That was weird. He was a friend. I wonder what changed him."

Holly shuddered. "He was scary." She pulled out the map. "Where do you think we are?"

SQUAARK.

A gull attacked through the mist, its beak aimed straight for Holly's eyes. At the last second it veered sideways and snatched away the map.

Holly clapped her hands over her face.

Owen stared upward in horror. "What's going on?"

A second and a third gull attacked in quick succession, diving at their faces and heads with piercing shrieks.

"Stop trying to blind us," yelled Owen. He leapt up, flailing his arms.

"Shhh, people will hear," gasped Holly. She was trembling.

Meow.

A white cat sprang in front of them and rubbed against Holly's knee.

"Manxie? Where did you come from?" Holly put out a hand.

The cat pulled away and padded deeper into the mist. It paused and turned its head. Green eyes stared.

Holly scrambled to her feet, bent double and followed. So did Owen.

The gulls attacked again and again, slamming their bodies, beaks and wings hard against the children.

Holly and Owen kept going, heads down, scuttling behind the cat.

The three ran through the castle, dodging in and out but always keeping to the thickest patches of mist.

The cat could avoid the searching humans, but it could not outwit the gulls. The Shades detected the tingling of magic even through the thickest patch of mist. They dove down again and again, terrorizing the children.

Owen's back and head were pecked and bruised.

Wicked beaks jabbed at Holly until her head ached. One beak scraped a groove along her temple and drew blood.

A wall loomed out of the fog.

The cat stopped at its base.

The birds attacked again.

Holly and Owen huddled against the stones, but the wall curved away and gave little protection. They crouched with their arms folded over their heads and faces, wondering why they had stopped there.

The cat crouched before them, watching for the next bird, ready to pounce.

The birds changed tactics.

Twelve gulls soared out of the mist and landed on the grass, just out of the cat's reach. They formed a silent menacing semicircle.

The birds stared at the cat and the children with avid red eyes.

The cat arched her back and hissed.

One bird clacked its beak. A second joined in. The others followed.

Beaks rattling like sabers, the gulls approached.

Holly and Owen shrank back.

"Why are the gulls so psycho?" whispered Owen. "This is insane."

Holly shook her head. "We need Earth Magic. Neither we nor the cat can win this on our own. Join me." Holly held out her hand. Owen grasped it. They closed their eyes and sent frantic mindspeak.

Help someone. Please help. We need Earth Magic. We're under attack.

Holly's memory sparked. She pointed at the gulls and yelled, "*Lhiat myr hoiloo*—to thee as thou deservest."

A dark shadow appeared on the wall behind them.

Snarling and growling filled the air.

Horrified, Holly and Owen swung around and staggered back.

A massive black dog took shape against the wall and sprang forward, red mouth gaping, gigantic teeth dripping and gleaming.

Brother and sister moved closer together.

"We're surrounded," said Holly.

"DROP!" yelled Owen and threw his weight against her.

The cat yowled as they tumbled on top of it.

The Black Dog leapt over them and killed two gulls.

Shrieking, the other birds rose through the blizzard of feathers and fled.

Crunching and growling, and shaking away feathers, the Moddy Dhoo ate its prey.

Sickened, Holly closed her eyes.

Owen pulled her to her feet. "Come on, Sis. We've reached the Round Tower. Where's the door? Let's get inside while that demon dog finishes dinner."

"Not so easy." Holly pulled herself together and pointed out the entrance high above their heads.

The cat wound around her ankles.

"Thanks for guiding us to the tower, Manxie," murmured Holly. She picked up the cat and gave it a hug. "Any ideas on how to reach the door? OUCH!"

The cat dug its claws into Holly's shoulder and sprang high in the air. It hung by front paws from the narrow ledge that formed the doorstep.

The children watched, poised to catch it.

The cat scrabbled with its hind legs until it found a footing on the wall and scrambled up.

It peered over the narrow ledge at the children.

Despite their anxiety, Holly and Owen grinned.

"No way, Jose," said Owen.

Looking affronted, the cat turned and scratched at the door.

It yawned open and a rope ladder tumbled down.

Baying loudly, the Moddy Dhoo leapt over Holly and Owen and disappeared into the tower after the cat.

Neither Holly nor Owen moved.

"What are you waiting for? More gulls?" said Manannan in an irritated voice. He leaned out and blew a handful of vervain and valerian pollen into the air.

A cloud of forgetfulness fell over the approaching archaeologists and castle staff. Looking bemused, they stopped and returned to the dig.

Owen swarmed up the ladder and Holly followed.

Inside the Round Tower, light glowed from Manannan's willow wand. "I bid you welcome, Magic Children, but there is no time to rest. Make haste. Climb quickly." He pointed to steps that spiraled up the inner walls of the Round Tower. "We must heal Ava."

Owen sighed. He was upset and tired and couldn't think straight. What was Ava doing at the Round Tower, and what was it with magic and dizzying heights?

Manannan beckoned.

Owen started toward the steps, too fatigued to argue.

Holly slumped against the wall. She wasn't sure she had any energy left. She needed to rest before coping with more surprises. She stared uneasily into the shadows. There was no sign of the big black dog.

Manannan chivied her along.

Holly and Owen trudged upward.

The Round Tower began to vibrate gently. The power increased as they ascended the column of stone. By the time they reached the top, the flags beneath their feet pulsed. The energy revived the children.

"It's circle magic," said Holly as she stepped out onto the flat roof. She leaned over the parapet and looked out at Pheric's Isle, peering through the mist veils. "The stone slabs we're standing on are arranged in a circle, the tower, the castle walls and the isle below each make a rough circle, encircled by another circle of breaking waves."

"Even the wind's circling around us," remarked Owen. "It's spiraling up and down the curves of the tower."

Manannan motioned them to one side. "Hurry, hurry! Ava is in need."

"Where is she?" asked Owen.

"Of course, my fault, my fault," tutted Manannan. "You are still in the real realm." He puffed his cheeks and blew.

Holly and Owen felt a slight jolt and a shift in light and time.

"Now you are with us." Myrddin and Equus appeared beside Holly. They nodded a welcome.

Owen ran to the White Horse and gazed at the small, still bird splayed on his back. "Ava, what's wrong with you?"

"She was touched by the Dark Shadow," Equus replied.

"You may lift her down and set her in the center of the floor."

Scared, Owen tenderly lifted the semiconscious hawk. She lay limply in his arms, but her eyes flickered. "Thank you," she said faintly.

As directed, Owen laid Ava in the center of the flat roof.

Myrddin turned to Manannan. "We need a shaft of light beamed through the Gates of Sunrise."

"The original purpose of this tower was to act as a beacon to channel light from the Place Beyond Morning," said Manannan. "Its magic is now awake, but the beacon will tear a hole in my cloak of mist. This will allow the Dark Being's eye to rest on Mann," he warned.

"The Dark Being will be here soon, whether or not we use the beacon," said Myrddin.

Manannan nodded. He began to pace the circumference of the tower roof and gestured for Myrddin, Equus, Holly and Owen to follow him. "Let your footsteps fall in the center of each stone slab," he instructed and began to chant:

"Light hold us, Light enfold us,
Light in our minds, Light for our times,
Enlighten this hour. Rekindle this tower,
Let Light glow, and grow, in each beating heart."

"Light hold us, Light enfold us...," repeated his followers.

"Light in our minds, Light for our times..." On they paced, chanting in unison as Manannan moved toward Ava.

From pockets in his garments, Manannan pulled twigs which he laid end to end around Ava.

"May the Tramman Tree protect you." He laid leafy sprigs on her breast. "The Bollan Bane bless you." He lifted his willow wand to point to the mist above them. "May the miracle of light surround and heal you."

The mist parted in a perfect circle. A pillar of sunlight beamed down, gilding Ava, and the entire top of the Round Tower.

The light was golden and warm filled with the fragrance of spring flowers. Holly and Owen, Equus and Myrddin closed their eyes, lifted their faces skyward and breathed deeply.

Manannan lifted his arms, as well as his face, and softly chanted incantations.

The stone flags grew warm. The crenellated parapet encircling them absorbed the sun. The ancient beacon charged with light.

Slowly, slowly, Ava changed shape.

The body of the tiny hawk lengthened and thickened. Feathers changed shape and color, wings furled and unfurled, the beak and eyes softened and became Ava's face. Her raven hair feathered again around her head, and the twist of silver containing the moonstone glowed once again upon her brow. She rose gracefully to her feet.

The radiant Hawkwoman bowed to Manannan, formally kissed both his cheeks, then turned to the Wise Ones, Holly and Owen.

"Thank you, friends. Without you I would have been

lost to the darkness." Ava's smile was brilliant. "But I am healed."

"Then we must take counsel," said Equus.

"Yes. We are besieged," said Myrddin. "The Lady's necklace is broken, and the Dark Being has captured Adam."

Equus and Ava winced.

"We will need our combined power to rescue him," said Ava slowly.

"I offer my power," said Manannan.

"Thank you." Myrddin bowed.

"Adam does not need rescuing!" A laughing voice echoed around the top of the tower. "I return him."

A body slid down the shaft of light and sprawled at their feet.

"Blimey," gulped Owen.

"Adam's dead," shrieked Holly. She ran and threw herself over his body.

"Hey, don't have a fit. I'm alive." Adam pushed Holly aside and struggled to sit up.

The laughter rang out again. "Sorry to be so abrupt, Adam. I took advantage of the unexpected situation."

Manannan and Myrddin intensified the beacon of light.

"Hide behind light while you can, Wise Ones," said the voice, still full of amusement. "Though I cannot look through it to see you, or enter your beacon, I have found you. Adam knows the truth. You cannot stop truth spreading. You cannot prevent darkness. It is always present.

"Light and Dark,
Dark and Light.

"Your suppression is at an end. The Dark rises. I am ready to take my full place again. Even you, the Wise Ones, will not be able to stop tonight's dark shadow. No one can."

Adam stared up, puzzled. What game was Doona playing now?

"Listen to Adam, Magic children. Adam is my emissary. Listen to him."

Holly clutched Adam's hands but turned her face up toward the voice. "Your emissary? Like Zorianna? Of course he's not," she stormed.

"All I ask is that you listen to him, child," said the Dark Being. "Remember, there are two sides to a tale." Her voice was light and reasonable.

Holly stared at Adam.

"It's true," Adam said. He let Holly help him to his feet. "There is another side to the story." He gestured toward the Wise Ones. "These guys threw her out when she was a kid. They nearly killed her."

The Wise Ones dropped their eyes and sighed.

CHAPTER NINE

A MAZE OF MINDSPEAK

Adam looked anxiously at his cousins. How could he make them understand that he was forced into being a double agent?

He racked his brain. He needed to say or do something that would give them a clue. Something subtle that wouldn't alert the Shade that the Dark Being had attached to him.

He'd not anticipated that.

He should have guessed that no matter how well he conned her, the Dark Being wouldn't trust him. How else was she using him!

Still, he'd bamboozled her all right. The Dark Being believed he was on her side. But he couldn't get rid of the Shade. It heard everything he said.

How could he alert his cousins?

Poor Holly and Owen. They looked shell-shocked.

Pity Chantel wasn't here. She knew him well and would pick up on odd behavior. He briefly wondered where she was, then went back to trying to get a coded message over to his cousins.

Adam stuck his hands in his pocket to stop them trembling. His fingers touched Ava's feather. His heart lightened, and he had the glimmerings of an idea.

He walked to the parapet, trying to look as though he hadn't a care in the world. He began to whistle a fragment of an old music hall song his dad sang—"Me and My Shadow."

Please get it, Holly. Get it, Owen, he thought.

※※※

"Is what Adam said true?" Holly's voice trembled. She looked accusingly at the Wise Ones. "Have you told us the whole truth about the Dark Being?"

"She's not the Dark Being. Her name's Doona. It means dark maiden," Adam tossed over his shoulder, then picked up whistling the same phrase over and over again.

Ava spoke. "What Adam says is true, but not interpreted truly. Doona was banished, but only as a last resort after her actions consistently put others in grave danger, life-threatening danger."

"She rescued me from danger," Adam said. "You didn't. She saved me." He stared intently at Holly. "This whole thing is a crock." He paused. "Doona is kind and beautiful. She helped me like Wendy helped Peter Pan." He stressed the last five words.

Holly looked puzzled.

Adam started whistling again.

Owen rolled his eyes. Adam was not making sense, and the whistling was irritating. It was a stupid tune. One his family sang when he was a little kid, always following his dad around the farm.

Adam whistled the same phrase over and over.

Owen clenched his fists. The words of the song were now stuck in his head. "Me and my shaaadow, walking down the avenuuue." They were repeating again and again. He couldn't stop them. His tired brain was acting like a stuck record.

"This situation is baffling," whispered Manannan to Myrddin. "Is the boy's head addled after his ordeal?"

Adam whistled more loudly.

Owen lost his temper. "Quit whistling and make sense Adam. We're about to be invaded by the Dark Being, no matter what you call her. You might not have been in danger, but Holly and I were. We've just been attacked by psycho gulls and a demon dog, and that was right here, not off in la la land."

Adam's back stiffened. He looked sideways at Owen, but kept on whistling.

"What's wrong, Adam?" said Holly. "We've been worried sick, desperate to find you. I'm glad the Dark Being...er Doona, saved you, but you must know she's bad news."

Adam whistled on and on.

"He's nuts." Owen made a gesture of despair. "The Dark Being's done his head in."

Adam swung round. "NUTS!…I'm not nuts…Just listen to me, you idiot." He grabbed Owen's shoulders and shook him hard. "Doona helped me. She helped me like Wendy helped Peter Pan."

Owen punched him on the nose.

Adam slumped to the ground.

The Dark Being's laughter rolled around the top of the tower. "So, war is already declared!"

Manannan cut off the shaft of light. Thunder clapped and torrential rain poured down.

"No!" cried Ava. "Light not Dark. Give us Light, for tonight will be very dark indeed."

Manannan's wand cracked for a second time.

The rain stopped and the cloak of mist vanished. The tower, Pheric's Isle and the entire Kingdom of Mann were bathed in glorious sunlight.

Ava sighed with relief.

Myrddin banged his staff on the flags and opened a portal.

<hr>

Adam, Holly and Owen landed with a THUD back in the real world. They sprawled on the floor of the living room at Castleview Inn, entangled with Myrddin's and Manannan's cloaks, arms and staffs.

Sunlight streamed in through the window.

Equus and Ava appeared in the corner.

Mr. Smythe stood by the stove with a tea kettle in his hand and a dropped jaw.

"Sorry about this, Smythe." Myrddin sorted himself out and helped Manannan to stand. "We need headquarters, and the children need some rest."

Mr. Smythe gulped and put the kettle on to boil.

Myrddin made introductions as though it was a normal gathering. "This is Manannan. Equus and Ava are in the corner. You have heard the children speak of them."

Still speechless, Mr. Smythe nodded politely to his strange guests.

The cousins scrambled to their feet, Adam pinching his bloody nose.

"Adam!" Mr. Smythe found his voice. He enfolded Adam in a bear hug that made bones crack and held him at arm's length. "Your nose! Who hit you!"

"Owen."

Mr. Smythe's face darkened.

Owen flushed. "I apologize, but the whistling was driving me mad," he said. "Need some ice?"

Adam nodded stiffly.

"Where's Chantel?" interrupted Mr. Smythe anxiously, suddenly realizing that another child was missing.

Myrddin held up his hand. "Chantel is safe, and Equus knows how to reach her." He turned to Equus. "She is alerting the Cabbyl Ushtey."

"She will be safe," confirmed Equus.

Mr. Smythe sighed and looked unhappy.

Holly sat quietly at the table, a puzzled frown still on her face. She stared at Adam, watching his every move as he and Owen found ice and a cloth and staunched the blood. Her frown cleared.

"She did some sewing for him," Holly said.

Adam's head shot up. His eyes looked hopeful.

"What?" said Owen.

A conversation between Mr. Smythe and Myrddin halted.

"Wendy...she did some sewing for Peter Pan. Right, Adam? So the Dark Being was like her, really helpful?"

Adam nodded, still holding the ice to his face. "She was kind. Just like Wendy," he mumbled.

Holly chose her words carefully. "So, you're like Peter Pan?" Holly hummed the tune that Adam had whistled.

Owen groaned and plugged his fingers in his ears. "Not that again, Holly."

Adam sighed with relief and grinned at Holly. "You've always been a smarty pants," he mumbled affably through the ice pack.

Holly pointed to her head and closed her eyes. *Can it read mindspeak?*

Adam shook his head and shrugged.

"Do you mind telling us what's going on?" said Owen.

"You're so dense sometimes," muttered Holly. She grabbed Mr. Smythe's notebook and pencil from the table, scribbled something and tore it out. She passed the note to Owen.

Wendy sewed a shadow onto Peter Pan's feet.
Adam's had a 'shadow' attached to him by the DB.
Watch what you say.

Owen's eyes widened. "It was a chick flick," he said. "Why would I know that?" He passed the note back to Holly and grinned at Adam. "How come you saw it?"

"I had to take Chantel for her birthday."

Both boys hooted with laughter.

"It's a book too, morons," said Holly. She retrieved the note, added a line, *Can it read our minds?* and passed the page over to Myrddin.

Myrddin read the note and gave a snort.

He gestured everyone to join him at the table and pushed the note across to Mr. Smythe.

Mr. Smythe read it and sighed. "I'm obviously missing something, but I understand."

Myrddin stuck the note in a pocket. "We need to plan," he said abruptly. "Gaia will be under attack tonight."

He sent a blast of mindspeak to everyone. *A Shade is shadowing Adam. It will report everything back to the Dark Being in her mindspeak.*

Humans mindspeak a different way. The Shade doesn't know they have that ability and cannot hear it. We will make a false set of plans using speech and another set using human mindspeak like I am doing now.

The kettle whistled. Everyone jumped.

"I think we need a cup of tea," said Mr. Smythe.

The Shade wriggled with delight. At lasst, planss! it thought. Human'ss converssationss with sstrange whisstling make no sensse. Planss do. The Dark Being wantss planss.

The Shade pooled contentedly beneath Adam's feet as he sat at the table.

"Manannan's fortress on Barrule is the obvious place from which to defend ourselves," said Myrddin. He switched to mindspeak. *We will make our stand on Pheric's Isle.*

"Then I will strengthen its defenses," said Manannan. *I will inform the Moddy Dhoo, but he is his own entity.*

"Oh, stop this," said Adam, playing his part to the hilt. "Doona won't hurt anyone if you reinstate her. Why fight her?" *She has an army of Shades. Masses of them.*

"Oh, shut up, Adam. No one believes the Dark Being except you." Owen turned to Myrddin. "But what's the point of us kids fighting? We can't do any real Magic." *I know how to get into Pheric's Isle without anyone seeing. That's where the secret passage goes. It comes out at the Round Tower.*

"You must not trust Doona, Adam. She is a problem you don't understand. Everyone needs to fight the darkness, even children," Myrddin rumbled. *Excellent, Owen.*

"I'm not fighting. Doona's my friend," said Adam. *Can you get rid of the Shade?*

"Doona is no one's friend," said Myrddin heavily. *Has it melded with you?*

"She's my friend. I'm not fighting her," replied Adam stubbornly. *No, it's attached as a shadow.*

"Then we will fight without you," said Myrddin. *Yes, I can detach it. But let the Shade deliver our false information first.*

"Did Doona send those psycho gulls that nearly killed us?" said Owen. *I thought the gulls were Manannan's?*

"Yes, Doona influenced my gulls. Her magic is stronger than mine," said Manannan. *Shades slipped in when Equus arrived. They discovered a way to meld with the gulls and enter Pheric's Isle. Be on your guard. Shades can meld with humans.*

"The Lady's death and loss of the beads is a terrible blow," said Ava. "It weakens us all, even Doona." *Holly must restring the beads and waken the Lady.*

"Without the Lady, we don't stand a chance against the Dark Being," said Holly. *I know where the beads are. I'll try to restring them tonight, but I need some thread. The Lady is a skeleton. Can she wake?*

"We must still fight the darkness; there is no one else," said Equus, tossing his mane and flicking his tail. A long white hair floated free and landed on the table near Holly. *The Lady will wake with the right Earth Magic when the necklace is complete. Use the hair from my tail as thread, Holly.*

Holly picked up the long hair. She curled and uncurled it around her finger.

"What will happen if she wins?" said Owen. *Don't forget to call the Lady using the secret rune name.*

"I can't believe we are having this conversation," interrupted Mr. Smythe. "This talk of a magic war is all nonsense. I'm having nothing to do with it." He leaned back, looking stubborn, folded his arms and closed his eyes. *Err...I hope this works. Never tried it before. I have some interesting information. I discovered the meaning of the runic name*

Cullyn in the museum. It's a very old form of Manx. It means Holly.

There was a long silence. Everyone looked at each other.

The Lady's secret name is Holly? said Owen.

So it seems, replied Mr. Smythe.

Wow.

Holly turned white. She stood up, swaying slightly. "I'm going for a nap. I can't take in anymore. No one's working with anyone else so we're going to lose the battle anyway. Adam's right. Negotiate with this Doona person so we don't have to fight. I'm exhausted. We hardly slept last night and today has been terrifying." She left the room. *Sorry, but I'm not kidding, I really am beat. I need some space to think about this. I don't know why, but it's a shock. I'm scared of what it means.*

Owen gave a big yawn and pushed his chair back. "Me too, Sis. I vote for not fighting. If you can't win, why fight? I didn't mind helping you Wise Ones get Tools, but this is daft. This fight is nothing to do with us." *I gotta rest too. I'll help when I'm not so beat, okay? Wake us before dark.*

"Humans are ungrateful," cried Ava, spreading her wings. "Maybe Gaia doesn't deserve to be saved." *Sleep and dream of Light, Magic Children. May Light always be in your hearts.*

Adam's Shade sent its first message to the Dark Being while watching the meeting break up in disarray. Adam heard it, but schooled himself not to react.

They fight amongst themsselvess. Jusst like you planned. Adam ssupportss you. The children are sscared. They don't wissh to fight. The Lady iss dead and the necklace broken.

The Wisse Oness will fight from a place called Barrule.

The Dark Being lost her temper. *The Lady dead? That cannot be!*

The ring on Adam's finger tightened painfully. He tried to ease it. As soon as he touched it Doona's words seared into his brain: *Find the broken necklace. Bring me the beads.*

Adam felt sick. The ring wasn't a gift. It conducted her messages. It hurt. It would make him do her bidding.

He twisted the ring and tried to remove it. The harder he pulled, the more painfully it gripped his flesh. He bent under the table and hissed to the shadow. "Tell her I don't know where the beads are. Ask her to stop hurting me, because it's true."

The Shade complied.

The ring slackened, then tightened again.

Find the beads before nightfall, roared Doona as Adam desperately pulled at the ring. *Someone knows where they are. If you don't find them, you'll die like the others.*

Adam felt sick. Doona had tricked him instead of him outwitting her.

Now he was caught. He daren't let Myrddin dispatch his shadow. Doona would know and punish him through the ring.

He was cornered.

Owen rapped lightly on the bedroom door and opened it a crack. "What's up, Sis?" he hissed.

"Don't call me Sis," replied Holly automatically. She blew her nose hard. "Come in."

Owen slid inside, quietly closing the door. He looked quizzically at Holly, who sat cross-legged at the head of her bed. "So, why are you so upset?"

Holly shook her head, but tears welled in her eyes. "The name. It was the last straw." She looked up at him. "You don't get it, do you?"

"Nope," said Owen cheerfully. He bounced up and down on the end of the bed. "Your mattress is softer than mine."

Holly hurled the pillow at him.

Owen caught it and grinned.

Holly glared.

Owen returned the pillow and lay back across the end of the bed, his hands behind his head. "Better spill the beans before you explode."

"It's feelings. Mixed-up feelings. I feel right at the center of everything, yet totally helpless. This situation's a mess."

"No. It's an onion."

Holly sat up straight. "Say that again."

"It's an onion," Owen repeated.

They both laughed.

"That's why it's making me cry." Holly blew her nose again.

"Haven't you realized what's happening, Holly? We're going round and round and coming to dead ends. Nothing seems connected. But each time something happens, we're getting closer and closer to the center. That's been happening right from the first adventure. We fix something, strip off a layer, and there is another underneath."

"All in circles. A real maze."

"Yup, like an onion."

"The Lady's the center."

"Yup."

"The name connects me to the Lady in a big way."

"Looks like it." Owen rolled over. "The sooner you string that darn necklace the better," he said seriously.

"I know." Holly gazed out of the window. "It's scary."

Outside was a scene from a postcard. The castle basked in brilliant sunshine. Its walls rose against a perfect blue sky and reflected in sparkling water. White gulls soared above, colorful boats floated below.

She sighed. "Earth Magic's shouting at me."

"Yup."

"It shouted at you? That's when you found the secret passage."

Owen nodded.

"I can use that passage to sneak in to thread the beads."

"Yup. Going to?"

"Coming with me?" she countered.

"You bet. I still need to make battle plans." He shifted on the bed. "Holly, do you trust Adam?" he asked abruptly.

Holly stared at the quilt. She sighed. "To be honest, I don't know. When he told us about Doona being thrown out when she was a kid, he was really sorry for her. He believed it. The way he said it made me feel sorry for her."

"Me too," muttered Owen. "I couldn't help thinking that's what happened to him. His mum kind of threw him and Chantel out when she packed them off to England."

"Ouch," said Holly. "I didn't think of that."

She paused. "What about the Wise Ones?" she said, her voice so low Owen could barely hear. "Do you trust them?"

"Whoa," said Owen. "That's some question." He thought for a while. "It changes everything."

Holly nodded. Her eyes bright with unshed tears. "I have to ask it. I'm being asked to resurrect really powerful magic. I...I...have to understand whose side I'm on."

"And whose side are you?" said Owen.

"Ours," whispered Holly. "You, me, Adam, Chantel and Mr. Smythe represent Gaia. I have to be on Gaia's side. I have to look out for us! I sense that Adam's right. The Wise Ones haven't told us everything. I...I still think they're good...but...I think they have a secret agenda, so I have to figure out what to do."

Shaken, Owen pulled the castle brochure containing the map out of his pocket. He consulted it. "The castle closes at six. We'll slip away then. According to Ava, there's less chance of the Dark Being bugging us while it's still light."

Holly stifled a yawn. "That gives us about an hour for a nap."

Owen took the hint and left.

Doona turned her ring.

She felt Adam's ring twitch in response. She smiled.

She had her hostage, and the great finale was in motion. She was ready. If the Lady was dead, she had nothing to fear.

She contacted the Shades gathered along the edges of the Mists of Time.

"Take heart. Gaia's sunlight is temporary. Watch carefully. In a few hours a great cosmic dark will begin. No one can halt it. As the sunlight fades, act as one body. Force your way through the Mists where they are weakest. Find me on Gaia. There you may unleash your anger and mayhem and punish the humans.

"I will deal with the Wise Ones as Gaia falls to its knees."

Adam pushed his chair back from the table and stood up.

"I'm going for a walk. I don't even know where I am, or what this place is called."

"Isle of Man," said Mr. Smythe.

"The Kingdom of Mann," said Manannan and the Wise Ones at the same time.

Everyone chuckled.

"Whatever! Is it a real place, or are we in a magical world? I don't even know how you got here or what day it is."

Myrddin clambered to his feet. "You are right, Adam. Forgive us. You must be really confused. We will take a walk, and I will explain. Much has happened since you were dragged into the mist."

They strolled along the River Nebb in the sunshine, the Shade flowing along at Adam's feet. Myrddin brought Adam up to date and pointed out many things: the plane, Mr. Cubbon crossing the road, the castle and the round tower. He also spoke carefully of the Kingdom of Mann and his long association with Manannan.

The Shade wiggled restlessly. None of this talk mattered. There was nothing here the Dark Being didn't know.

Under cover of their conversation Adam showed Myrddin his finger. *I've messed up again, Myrddin. Doona said the ring was a gift, so I accepted it. But it's torturing me, trying to make me do what she wants.* The ring had bitten deeply into his flesh. The finger was red and swollen.

Myrddin's face grew grave. *What is it she asks?*

That I find the beads and give them to her. The Shade told her the Lady is dead. So she wants the beads now, before anyone else gets them. Adam cradled his hand. *I don't know where the beads are, so how can I get them? But she won't stop hurting me.*

Myrddin looked sad. *The Shade I can deal with, but not the ring. It is linked with Doona's ring and under her control. Tell the Shade you've worked out that it's Holly who knows where the beads are, but she's sleeping. The Shade knows that's true. Promise to follow Holly when she wakes.*

Adam nodded. He ran ahead of Myrddin, as though

attracted by the Viking boats in the river, and whispered to the Shade.

It immediately sent mindspeak to the Dark Being.

The ring eased on Adam's finger.

Adam sighed with relief. He'd bought some time.

***

As Holly napped, she dreamed a dream that she had dreamed before. A dream she'd almost forgotten. This time the dream was clearer. Now it made sense.

Holly flew over a silver sea toward a castle on a small island. From the castle's center rose a tall round tower. She recognized Pheric's Isle and swooped over the castle walls.

A figure stood on the circular platform at the top of the round tower, a cloaked figure in a long green skirt. One arm was outstretched, and silver threads of magic spun from the fingers creating a delicate web of light that spiraled to the stars. The other hand clutched a glowing necklace.

"Who are you?" shouted Holly. "Pease tell me." She dived down.

The figure looked up.

Holly felt the same flash of recognition she'd had in the earlier dream. She'd seen those eyes before. Now she knew why. Her own eyes looked back at her! She was seeing her future.

***

Holly woke from the dream with her heart pounding. She lay on the bed trying to figure out its significance. The image stayed clear in her mind, its details compelling.

"Earth Magic," she muttered as she rose. "I'd better listen." She opened her backpack and pulled out a garment that had been rolled up and thrust in the bottom—a dark green skirt.

Her mother had thrust it in at the last minute. "In case Mr. Smythe takes you to a posh restaurant." Holly had laughed and protested, but her mother had insisted.

Holly unrolled the skirt. It looked like the one in her dream.

She slipped out of her jeans and put it on.

The full skirt had deep pockets. She filled them with what she needed.

※※※※

Owen catnapped for about twenty minutes, then sneaked out of Castleview Inn to look for Mr. Cubbon.

The old fisherman was sitting at his usual table outside the pub, enjoying the sunshine and a pint of beer. He beamed and waved.

"Good afternoon, young man. 'Tis a fine afternoon and evening after all."

Owen looked around with raised eyebrows. No one else seemed to be enjoying it. Raised voices were coming from a large group by the door. He slid into the seat farthest away from them and observed the old man.

Mr. Cubbon sipped his beer and leaned forward. "How's the magic goin', boy?" he whispered.

"Er, brilliant. I mean..." Owen was rattled. This Mr. Cubbon was a far cry from the man who had accused them in the castle. "That is..." Owen decided to be blunt.

"Why did you accuse Holly of stealing?"

The beer mug slammed down, slopping half its contents onto the table. "I never did. Not in this life. What are yer talking about?"

Owen checked around. No one was near enough to overhear. He leaned across the table. "Did you go inside Peel castle this afternoon?"

The old man frowned and rubbed his forehead. "Well. I did and I didn't." He told a strange tale of feeling ill, having memory blanks, and finally coming to inside the castle and being shouted at by the ticket collector. "In a fine old paddy, she was. Saying I'd bin rude and caused trouble. So I left. Don't know what made me go in the castle. Don't know what trouble I caused."

Owen grinned. "You caused a rumpus, but I don't think it was your fault. Remember those strange shadows you saw when we arrived?"

Mr. Cubbon nodded.

"They're called Shades. I think one possessed you, melded with you for a short time. You didn't have the flu. It was the Shade. It made you do stuff." He gestured to the group arguing. "I think it's the Shades' influence that's making everyone so aggressive."

The old fisherman blenched and pushed back his chair. "Well, I'm not having that 'appen again. There's old Manx charms to fix that kind a thing. I'll be going to set them up."

Owen leaned forward. "Wait. I've an idea," he whispered.

They talked quietly together.

Mr. Smythe looked uneasily at the three strange beings across from him. Never in his life had he imagined such a scene. Nothing he had learned, not even his years as a historian exploring wondrous things, had prepared him for this moment.

He sipped his tea and tried to pretend it was quite normal to be in the room with a mythical horse, a strangely beautiful Hawkwoman and a sorcerer.

"Forgive us. We are usually more careful about how we appear to humans." It was Ava who spoke. "Would you rather we were just a presence you could sense?"

Mr. Smythe replaced his cup in the saucer with a clatter. "No, no," he said quickly. "I'd rather see. There's been too much going on I've not seen."

Ava smiled. "You are a wise man."

Mr. Smythe felt her approval. It eased his heart.

"You are worried about the child Chantel?" It was the horse who spoke this time.

Mr. Smythe's throat tightened. He gave a sharp nod.

"Myrddin has protected her. She is the youngest and most vulnerable. He gave her a task that keeps her safe until the Dark comes. She is with the Cabbyl Ushtey, the white horses of the sea. Her affinity is horse magic. They will care for her, delight her and keep her out of danger until the last moment when they are needed. The child was grieving for her lost brother and could not take any more uncertainty. The Cabbyl Ushtey will bring her to Pheric's Isle when they are called."

"Thank you." Mr. Smythe cleared his throat. "And when they are called, when the Dark comes?"

"When the Dark comes, none of us will be safe," said Equus sadly.

Manannan bowed deeply. "Which is why we must take our leave and prepare. We are deeply grateful for your hospitality. But please excuse us."

All three beings bowed.

Manannan's cheeks puffed, and a great wind swirled through the room.

Mr. Smythe was alone again, feeling scared and inadequate.

He wandered over to the window and stared at his plane bobbing on the incoming tide. His skills were practical ones like flying, sorting through old manuscripts or sticking ancient pots together. They were of little use in this situation.

"Hey, Mr. Smythe...MR. SMYTHE!"

The call came from the street below.

Owen and Mr. Cubbon were staring up, beckoning him to join them.

CHAPTER TEN

LIGHT AND DARK

The cavernous cellar under Castleview Inn was a mess, but there were no worries about someone hearing the children falling over things. A rock band was playing in the pub above them, and a fight had broken out.

BOOM, BOOM, BUBBA, BUBBA, BOOM, beat the drummer.

Beams shook, floorboards vibrated and a crash and scrape that sounded like a fallen chair made Holly jump. Dust motes filled the air so the one dim lightbulb became even dimmer.

Holly looked at the rubbish and rubble in dismay. No wonder Owen had been covered in cobwebs after his explorations. She wished she had kept her jeans on. She began to work her way across the floor to the dark hole in the far wall.

Owen and Mr. Cubbon clattered down the stairs behind her.

Both hauled sacks.

"It's turning nasty up there," said Owen. "We could have marched an army through and no one would have noticed." He eyed her skirt. "Who are you trying to impress? The Shades?" He and Mr. Cubbon guffawed.

Holly ignored his comment. "What's with the sacks? Isn't there enough rubbish down here?"

Owen grinned and stuck his arm inside. "TAA-DAA." He flung a fluorescent green bike helmet over to Holly. "Chosen to go with your skirt."

She caught it. "Ooooh, good taste little bro'. Protection from the gulls?"

"Yup. Plus we don't know how low the passage roof goes."

"Good idea." Holly buckled it on.

"Am I what is known as 'cool'?" enquired Mr. Cubbon through the visor of a purple bike helmet.

"Very cool." Holly grinned, then laughed out loud as Owen produced a miner's helmet, complete with lamp. "Where did you get this stuff?"

"I have connections," said Mr. Cubbon.

Owen passed out flashlights. "Loop the string around your neck, so you can't drop them. But don't bang them on rocks, or the bulb will go." He tied a knot in his sack and slung it over his shoulder. "Hey ho, hey ho, and off to work we go." He switched on the helmet lamp and stepped into the secret passage.

It was dark and dusty but well made and wide enough

for all three of them to walk together. Brickwork walls solidly arched above. Cobbled ground fell gently away.

"Definitely a smugglers' passage," grunted Mr. Cubbon. "Wide enough for a pony carrying barrels of brandy, see?" He stopped to cough. "Too much dust. I can't talk and walk."

"At least it's dry," said Holly. She'd had visions of slimy mud and seaweed.

Their flashlights created a wide beam that cut comfortingly through the dark, and they walked with increasing confidence. The tunnel dipped under the river estuary, then rose gently on the other side where the brick walls gave way to solid rock.

The passage suddenly turned to the left and began to slope down again.

"Listen," said Holly. "I hear the sea."

"Then it goes to the smugglers' cave, way out beyond Fenella Beach. We don't want that way," said Mr. Cubbon.

Holly and Owen cast their light beams around.

"There isn't another way," Holly said at last.

"Aye, there is. The raven told me. Never been wrong yet." Mr. Cubbon nudged Owen. "You magicked the passage last time. I reckon you better magic it again."

"It might take a while." Owen swung down his sack and balanced his helmet on top so the beam shone on the wall. He placed both hands on the rock face and leaned into it, his ear flat against the surface.

Owen closed his eyes and concentrated, trying to forget Holly's and Mr. Cubbon's anxious faces.

It took a few minutes, but he finally caught it.

The slow distant pulse came from deep in the ground.

Deeper than he'd ever heard before. He listened until the heartbeat of the rock pulsed through him. His heartbeat slowed. He became part of it.

"Rock," he whispered, "may I use your Earth Magic? Please show me the passage to the Round Tower. The Lady needs our help."

He listened, then motioned to Holly and Mr. Cubbon.

"It wants to know your hearts too. Place your hands and cheek against the wall. Listen for a long slow heartbeat."

"Like we did with the standing stones at Avebury?" said Holly, unbuckling her helmet. She pressed against the rock.

Mr. Cubbon copied their actions. "I'm a little deaf," he said as he leaned into the rock.

"Use your Magic Ear," said Owen.

They closed their eyes and listened.

At the same moment, all knew they could enter.

They exchanged shining glances and stroked their thanks on the surface of the wall.

It dissolved beneath their hands.

The flashlights revealed a narrow stone staircase that spiraled up into darkness.

"It's ancient," said Owen in awe. "Look how the center of each step has been worn away." He placed one foot on the bottom step to demonstrate. It fitted the worn hollow. He looked up at the steps circling above him. "We're going to need those helmets, and it will be a pain dragging up the sacks. You better go first, Holly."

Round and round they climbed, losing track of time, unable to see ahead because of the curves, fumbling with feet and hands, taking breaks when Mr. Cubbon's panting became too loud.

"Daylight!" yelled Holly.

One by one, they emerged from the shadows into the large circular room halfway up the tower. Sunlight slanting through slits in the walls illuminated the wooden door. The rope ladder lay at its base.

"Ready to face the gulls, Holly?"

Holly tightened her helmet and nodded.

"Then give us a minute."

Owen squatted by the door and opened his sack.

He took out plastic bags full of smooth pebbles and two slingshots and laid them ready.

"You're going to kill the gulls? Kill the Shades?" Holly was shocked.

Owen shook his head, "I don't think that's possible. They're magical. So I'm using Earth Magic to stun them. Then Myrddin and the others can figure out what to do with them."

Mr. Cubbon produced a bag full of green plants. "Tuck Bollan Bane in one pocket and rowan in the other," he said. Next he handed out garlic cloves. "Rub these on the bottom of them shoes." He rummaged again in the sack and found a plastic spray bottle full of water. "Charmed this, I did." He sprayed both the children and the pebbles. "Fetched the water meself from Spooyt Vane, the magic white spout. Now if that lot doesn't keep the nasties from melding I dunno what will." He grinned. "And I got more charms for backup."

"Thank you, Mr. Cubbon," said Holly. She patted his arm and took a deep breath. "Now or never."

Together they lifted the thick wooden bar and eased the door open.

They peered through.

The castle was closed and deserted. The evening sun cast long shadows from the ruined walls over the grass. Nothing stirred other than the circling gulls.

Holly eyed them nervously.

Owen pulled the door wide open.

Mr. Cubbon tossed down the rope ladder and helped Holly over the edge.

Owen sat in the doorway, slingshot poised. "Gull number one approaching," he warned.

Holly tensed. Keeping her face to the wall, she concentrated on descending, rung by unsteady rung.

She felt the displacement of air as the gull swooped toward her.

THWACK. It fell to the ground stunned. The first of Owen's stones had found its mark.

"Well done, boy."

They watched carefully. The Shade possessing the gull didn't seem to emerge.

"I knew charmed water would do the trick," said Mr. Cubbon.

"Two gulls at two o'clock," called Owen.

THWACK. THWACK. Subdued cheers.

"There's a group coming in together," warned Mr. Cubbon.

He was right. Three gulls slammed Holly with wings

and beaks. Another fell to the ground, courtesy of the sharpshooters.

Holly doggedly felt for another rung on the swaying ladder.

"You're nearly down," Owen called to her.

Holly touched the grass as another group of gulls attacked, each from a different direction. She huddled against the wall. The attack was bad, but the helmet saved her.

"They're getting smart," said Owen.

Mr. Cubbon snorted and picked one off as it flew away.

"Five down. That's a start." Owen stuffed his pockets full of charmed pebbles and half swung, half slid down the ladder. "I'll cover Holly, if you hold the fort, Mr. Cubbon."

"That I will, I will." Mr. Cubbon sat in the middle of the doorway, visor shining, legs dangling, slingshot armed. "I've not had this much fun in years." He tossed down one of the sacks. "Don't forget this."

Owen thrust the sack at Holly. "Go on, leg it."

They ran the gauntlet of the gulls, down the grassy slope, around a battlement, through an archway to the archaeologists' hut. One gull fell to Mr. Cubbon, but the rest were too far away for his shots to reach.

"It's locked. I should have known." Holly thumped on the door in frustration.

Owen pulled out his Swiss pocketknife and opened the spike as the gulls mounted another attack. He passed it to Holly. "You do it. I'll shoot."

She picked frantically at the lock. It wouldn't give.

Gulls bombarded the children in swift formation.

Owen, ducking as well as shooting, missed them all.

He changed his tactics. He stared without flinching until the first gull was almost upon them. Then he let fly.

"Bull's-eye," he crowed and ducked.

He couldn't reload fast enough. He and Holly suffered the next few assaults cowering in the doorway.

"I'll try that again. Yeah. Eight down!"

Holly rattled the padlock in frustration.

"Cool it, Sis."

Taking deep breaths and clearing her mind of the fear and distractions, Holly held the lock in both hands, willing it to open. She envisaged the catch inside and mentally asked it to move.

The hasp sprang open.

Unlatching the door she leapt inside. Owen grabbed the sack and followed, slamming the door behind him.

"Only three psycho gulls left," he said.

Holly was riveted by the beads.

Owen pulled two small prickly branches from Mr. Cubbon's sack. He laid one on the window ledge, opened the door and slid one across the threshold.

"What are they?" said Holly without looking up.

"Holly boughs," replied Owen. "Mr. Cubbon said to put them around the Lady's grave. He knows a lot of Earth Magic. He says they're Manx charms."

Holly turned her head, eyes wide. "That's tree magic: 'Holly boughs strewn at entrances keep dark magic at bay.'

The Mother Tree told me that in the second adventure. I'd forgotten. Thanks."

"Do you need to be on your own now?"

"Yes, please," said Holly softly.

"Holler if you need me." Owen slipped outside with the sack.

He sat in the doorway, picking off the psycho gulls, one by one. As the last one hit the dust, he left the doorway and ran until he could see Mr. Cubbon. He waved.

Mr. Cubbon returned the wave.

"We got the lot," Owen bellowed.

"I'll be headin' back then."

Owen watched as the old fisherman pushed the door of the round tower almost shut, wedging a rowan twig in the crack so it didn't latch.

⁂

The castle was silent and full of beauty. The tips of the ruined walls were touched with gold sunlight; the shadows lay in interesting patterns.

Owen worked silently, laying the holly boughs, rowan twigs and Bollan Bane around Breesha's grave.

Manannan's gulls soared peacefully on the air currents, occasionally diving into the sparking water of the bay.

A splashing of oars and laughter reached him from the river estuary.

The sun sank lower and the quality of light gradually changed.

There was a heaviness, a darkness, a feeling of fear in the air.

The laughter from the boats on the estuary took on a cruel edge and dissolved into yells and insults.

Owen looked up. It was way before sunset. Darkness shouldn't be here yet.

The sun was a dull orange globe with the hint of a bite out of one side.

Owen held his hands up to his eyes to cut out the brightness. He squinted through the tiny gaps between his fingers.

The bite grew as he watched.

Doona's words rang in his ears. "Even you, the Wise Ones, will not be able to stop tonight's dark shadow. No one can."

Doona was causing an eclipse of the sun.

The terror had begun.

<hr />

Holly switched on the lamp and stared at the tray full of beads. They were utterly beautiful.

A curl of fright fluttered. The black bead wasn't there. Then she spotted it, off to one side in a container.

She pulled the horse hair from her pocket. She knew how the necklace started. Picking up the large amber disk, she threaded it, and with a sigh of relief slid the jet black bead next to it. Dark and Light were together again.

It was like picking up fries fresh from the oven. The beads had a magical heat, an electricity all their own, that prickled on her fingers and palms.

She stopped and pulled out a stool. She needed to sit and concentrate.

Holly laid her hands above the hair and beads already strung as though she were blessing them. She closed her eyes and tried to recall her dream, to freeze the image when Breesha's necklace had spilled out of Mona's ripped tunic. That was the moment the glowing beads had seared into her memory.

Her heart pounded, her hands shook.

She could feel the magic. The beads were so powerful that she wasn't sure she should touch them.

She pulled her trembling hands away.

If not you, then who?

The voice was as soft as a breath of wind.

"Is that you, Lady?"

Silence.

Holly worked to center herself.

From her pockets she pulled a tea light and a match folder, a rock from the beach, a phial of water and a feather. She placed them around the tray.

Singing softly she lit the candle.

"Earth support me,
 Air surround me,
 Fire enlighten me,
 Water cleanse me."

She sang it over and over, rocking slightly back and forth. At last she closed her eyes, held her hands over the beads and waited.

The vision came.

Her fingers moved of their own accord, deftly toward a

silver bead, eagerly toward the malachite. Red glass slipped against turquoise, a gold disk against a pale blue crystal. Her fingers worked first on one side of the amber disk, then on the other. The necklace grew.

The vision in her head changed.

Holly saw the moment when Sigurd held the necklace up before placing it around Breesha's neck.

Her fingers flew faster. She must finish the back of the necklace before the vision vanished.

White glass, brown clay, rose quartz, topaz, rough lapis lazuli, silky tiger's eye, green glass, cobalt and a pure gold nugget.

She knotted the ends.

Breathless, she opened her eyes and looked at the fabulous links that lay across her palms.

"The Lady holds the entire universe around her neck." Was that what Myrddin had said?

Now she, Holly, held it in her hands.

The scent of roses filled the air, but darkness thickened in the corner of the hut. A growl rumbled.

***

Myrddin and Adam leaned over the bridge rail, staring down at the River Nebb. Both were distracted.

Myrddin was mindspeaking to Equus and Ava.

Adam, his hand in his pocket, was trying to ignore his throbbing finger.

He was in a black depression.

He thought he'd done his best. He thought he'd outwitted the Dark Being. Instead she had outwitted him.

Once again he'd done everything wrong.

Holly and Owen couldn't be with him because of the Shade, and now the ring was trying to force him to take the beads.

His finger ached.

He tried to distract himself by staring at a group of men boarding the Viking longboats to practice rowing. They needed practice. The enormous oars were hard to handle and there was much splashing and good-natured hurling of insults as the ships floated downstream.

Adam, deep in his misery, didn't notice the changing light. People streamed past him, pointing at the sun. They gathered along the harbor with dark glasses and homemade eye shades.

As the light grew more ominous, the rivalry between the boats became pronounced. What had started as fun became nasty. One man lost his temper and whacked the arm of an opponent with his oar.

The ensuing fight jolted Adam back to reality. He nudged Myrddin.

"Yes. She approaches and even the most peaceful will become aggressive."

Both stared up at the sun.

The ominous orange globe hung low in the sky. The dark bite in its side slowly obscured its light.

"She's not waiting for dark; she's making the dark," said Adam, horror in his voice.

Again the ring constricted painfully around his finger.

GET THE BEADS NOW, came Doona's order.

Adam yelped. His finger tuned blue. "What am I going to do? What am I going to do?"

"Hold my staff." Myrddin had never sounded so stern.

Adam held on. The constriction and pain abated a little as he felt the staff's magic course through his hand.

"The Dark is here. The Shade has outstayed its usefulness." Myrddin scattered stardust on Adam's shadow.

With a soundless yell the Shade detached from Adam, writhed on the ground for a moment and fled into the air.

Though his hand still hurt, Adam felt easier. At least he could now talk to his cousins.

Myrddin stamped his staff. "A portal, Manannan, a portal."

Mr. Smythe waited by the harbor steps with another of Mr. Cubbon's sacks. He watched the black disk eating into the livid sun.

"Aye, it's begun," said Mr. Cubbon as he joined Mr. Smythe.

The two men rowed out to the plane, keeping plenty of sea room between them and the warring Viking boats.

Adam and Myrddin landed in the center of Pheric's Isle.

The Myrddin's disguise was shed. His staff crackled and sparked at every move. His billowing cloak glinted with magical colors.

Ava appeared beside him, towering over them all, wings unfurled, hawk eyes watchful, a strange and terrifying sight.

Equus galloped down from the sky, tail and mane streaming, his white coat shimmering with starlight.

Adam shielded his eyes.

A hand tugged Adam's arm. "Step back, Adam. They have forgotten how fearful they appear." Manannan sheltered the boy with his cloak.

"The hour has come. The real world and the realm of magic must fuse." Myrddin pointed his staff at the outer walls of the castle. They shimmered and rebuilt as the ancient ones aeons ago intended, concealing the inner magic from the human eyes without.

Myrddin pointed his staff at the Round Tower. It charged with light.

They approached the Lady's grave.

Holly, eyes cast down against the Wise Ones' brightness, waited for them, the glowing necklace looped through her fingers. She quivered with tension. She had no idea what she had to do.

Owen crouched beside the hut, preparing something in his sack.

Everything seemed insubstantial in the dimming light from the sun.

The fear in the air was real.

※

"Adam," hissed Owen.

Adam peered round the edge of Manannan's cloak.

Owen was half hidden by the hut wall. "Dumped the Shade yet?" His voice was urgent.

Adam nodded.

Owen beckoned him over. "Then help me make more ammunition before all hell lets loose." He was swiftly wrapping pebbles in Bollan Bane leaves and clipping them in place with small rubber bands.

"What's it for?"

"The Shades. It won't kill them, but Bollan Bane's Earth Magic. I'm hoping it will distract them."

I'M COMING. ADAM, GET THE BEADS.

Adam's ring tightened. He stumbled and clutched his hand to his chest. His face was white.

Owen grabbed his hand and looked at it. "Heck. Can't you get the ring off?"

"No. It's Doona's."

Owen grabbed his knife. He tried to insert a tiny blade between the finger and ring.

HOW DARE YOU? roared Doona.

"Owen, NO, stop," Adam groaned. He sank to the ground, his eyes rolling back as the ring bit to the bone.

Scared, Owen dropped the knife but sprinkled Adam's hand with the water from Spooyt Vane, and pressed a Bollan Bane leaf over the ring.

Adam opened his eyes as the pain abated a trifle. He clambered to his feet. "I can't help you. She won't let me, I-I'm sorry."

He staggered toward the Lady's grave.

A sad sweet song filled the castle grounds. The sounds were meaningless, yet everyone around the grave understood.

The Lady was singing the magical rune song.

"Lady, Lady, we hear your voice, please come to us. I've restrung your necklace. We have need of you." Holly knelt at the head of the grave and held out the necklace.

The bones gleamed dully.

The song continued.

A child's voice joined in. It came from a great distance but drew closer amid a galloping of hooves and the smell of the sea.

Chantel, on the back of a young Cabbyl Ushtey, cantered across the grass. Water droplets studded her skin and hair like diamonds. As she rode she sang a reply to the Lady's song.

The young Cabbyl Ushtey stopped, and Chantel slid off its back. She ran to the graveside and flung out her arms, scattering drops of sea water over the bones. "Lady, the Cabbyl Ushtey rejoice to hear your voice. They send their blessings." Chantel scattered more water. "She's singing about her lost name again," she whispered to Holly. "She needs to hear it."

Holly laid the necklace over the bones. She took a deep breath.

"Cullyn, Cullyn, I call your name. I am the child from the future you saw in your dream.

"Cullyn, Cullyn, I know your name.

"Holly in my language, Cullyn in yours.

"Your name is my name; my name is yours.

"Cullyn, I hear you and I've restrung your necklace.

Please help us. Doona and the Darkness are here."

A faint light materialized at the foot of the grave.

A woman wearing a simple brown cloak and a dark green skirt flickered in and out of the air like a flame.

"Lady!" The Wise Ones knelt.

"Kneel not," said the woman softly, "but listen well. For though I am called, I choose not to permanently return in my true form."

Holly turned a startled face toward the Wise Ones.

Chantel's hand trembled in Holly's.

"It's a crock, Holly. I told you it's all a crock. This isn't our war." Adam stumbled to her side. "Don't play along. They're forcing us to do their dirty work."

Darkness thickened between Adam and the Lady.

The Moddy Dhoo snarled and bared its teeth.

"TAKE THE NECKLACE, ADAM."

Everyone heard Doona's voice.

Adam clutched his finger and writhed in agony but yelled a defiant, "NO."

His ring hand moved of its own accord toward the beads.

He thrust it toward the Black Dog's mouth.

"Don't be daft!" yelled Owen and rugby-tackled Adam. They both rolled into the grave.

The Moddy Dhoo howled a terrible howl of disappointment as the offering was snatched away.

Holly grabbed the necklace before the boys rolled over it. She disappeared in a flash of light.

At the same instant, Chantel slapped the Cabbyl Ushtey's rump. "Go," she cried. "You know what has to be done."

The water horse leapt over the walls.

Doona appeared by the grave. The boys froze at her feet. She turned her ring. Thousands upon thousands of Shades appeared and silently circled, beginning the vortex.

Myrddin's staff, Ava's circlet and Equus's talisman crackled into a blaze of light.

Doona tossed her black hair and laughed. The one white hair caught in her curls glinted as she bent forward and dragged Owen and Adam in front of her as a shield.

The black disk overtook the sun. A spurt of light flickered around the edges and a gray pall settled over Gaia.

"Give me the necklace or forfeit these lives," crowed Doona.

The only sound was the drone of a passing plane. The engine drone changed to a high-pitched buzz as the plane swooped overhead.

Everyone looked up.

Charmed water rained down as Mr. Cubbon sprayed super soaker after super soaker through the open door.

"Way to go, Mr. Cubbon!" yelled Owen. He pulled a handful of Bollan Bane from his pocket and rubbed it in the Dark Being's face.

She dropped his arm. Juice from the leaves stung her skin and made her eyes water. She struggled to clear them with one hand.

Her grip on Adam tightened.

Owen melted into the background and found his sack. He was well covered with Mr. Cubbon's charms, and the Shades shrank back.

The plane passed overhead again.

Garlic cloves and water balloons showered down, causing havoc among the Shades.

The vortex broke apart.

Owen leapt around, waving saltshakers. He circled the Wise Ones and the grave, shaking the salt in a wide path.

The Shades pressed to the edge but advanced no farther.

"Stop this childish nonsense." Doona shook with rage. "I still have the boy." She dragged Adam to his feet.

"And I have the necklace," called out a clear voice.

Everyone turned.

The Lady appeared at the top of the Round Tower. She wore the beads.

The tower pulsed with light.

The Lady stretched out a hand, pulled threads of light from the tower and threw them toward the sky.

Stars gleamed.

She pulled more light from the tower and threw it toward the sun.

The disk of darkness began to move. A sliver of gold appeared on one side.

She pulled another handful of light and paused, looking down at Doona and the others.

The hood fell back.

"It's Holly," whispered Adam. "Where did she get the cloak?"

An awestruck silence fell.

"The cloak and necklace have passed," said the Lady. She stood at the head of the grave beside Doona. Without her cloak, her features could be clearly seen.

Both women stood in the same attitude: heads thrown back, gazing up at the tower. Both had flowing manes of hair, one dark, one white.

Holly looked down at the women and felt the magical beads stir. They brought her a vision. Two sisters, almost at one in age and blood, fighting for supremacy. For a second, Holly felt the intensity of a younger sister's jealousy and her hatred of the accident of birth that gave her less power. She felt the older sister's love and pity and guilt, and suddenly she understood the situation before her.

"You are not just sisters," said Holly. Her voice traveled clearly in the silence. "Light and Dark, Dark and Light. You are magical twins. Your role is to balance one another."

The Wise Ones gave a sigh like the wind. They lowered their Tools of Power.

"I have the boy," said Doona.

Holly raised the hand holding the light toward Doona. "Let Adam go," she said. "Your fight is not with him."

Doona laughed.

Holly opened her fingers. "*Lhiat Myr HIloo*—To thee as though deservest."

Minute sparks answered from the white hair entangled in Doona's curls. Doona gasped. She let go of Adam and held her head. "How are we connected?" she shouted to Holly. "It is not possible! I renounced all light."

Adam stumbled toward Myrddin.

"Take off your ring," Holly's voice was implacable.

Doona jutted her chin.

The white light around her grew stronger. The Moddy

Dhoo appeared on one side of the beam, the white cat on the other.

"Dark and Light, Light and Dark," said Holly softly. "The balance of power." She held out the necklace. "I restrung your bead, Doona. It lies again beside the Lady's amber disk as it should. Light and Dark. Dark and Light. I restored the balance that you denied." Her voice dropped to a whisper, yet all could still hear. "I hold the power."

No one argued.

"Adam said this wasn't our war. He is right. The people of Gaia never asked for the Tools of Power to come here. The Lady chose Gaia as their hiding place.

"Lady, you chose not to fight with your sister, which seemed good. But you involved Gaia. You brought your problems here.

"Equus told us the Wise Ones could not interfere among humans. Unwittingly you did.

"Doona, this isn't our war. I give you another chance to keep the balance.

"The Lady has let the necklace pass.

"Let Adam go. Let the Shades go. And let your ring of power pass."

"Come, Doona." The Lady spoke. She held out her hand across the grave. "The child is wise. Our place is no longer on Gaia. Be not afraid to enter the Mists. Our time has come and our magic must pass. We can go together, you and I. Together as we used to be. Light and Dark, Dark and Light, as time began. Before our Tools came between us."

Doona's hand moved slowly toward her ring.

The Shades rustled and quivered.

Mist rose from the ground, and two shining doorways appeared, one filled with luminous white mist and soft runesong, one with a billowing dark.

"No." Doona's did not waver. She spun her ring, forcing the Shades to spin themselves into a vortex once again.

Adam screamed.

"Then I have no choice." Holly's voice broke on a sob.

She laid the necklace across the parapet, pulled out her flashlight and, holding it like a hammer, smashed the jet black bead.

Doona's cry was piteous.

The stone in her ring shattered into fragments. She slumped to the ground, visibly fading away.

Adam fainted. Myrddin caught him. All watched as his arm fell loose. The shattered ring slipped off his finger and rolled into the grave.

Cullyn lifted her twin to her feet.

Doona was as insubstantial as her sister.

Singing softly, an arm lovingly around her, Cullyn guided Doona toward the doorways.

At the last moment, Cullyn looked up at Holly.

"You are wiser than I," she called. "I could not find the heart-courage to smash my twin's bead and sever her from magic. I had not the strength to send her into the Mists before her time.

"Instead I directed concealment of the Tools and hid myself, hoping to end her jealousy.

"It was a poor decision that caused untold misery in the universe. I choose to restore the balance. To relinquish my magic and enter the Mists." She turned to Doona. "Light and Dark, Dark and Light. There is always a choice, Doona."

"Then there must always be Dark," whispered Doona. "The Dark is as beautiful as the Light. I go willingly to the Dark. Grieve not, Sister. Chosen dark is peaceful oblivion."

They embraced and each stepped through different doors.

Sunlight returned.

Applause rippled over the walls from the people watching the eclipse outside the castle.

Inside the walls there was stillness and sadness.

"Uh-oh," muttered Owen, eyeing the mass of Shades beginning to drift aimlessly through the air. "How do we get rid of them? I've run out of salt."

Chantel whistled.

With the sound of waves crashing on the shore, a herd of Cabbyl Ushtey leapt over the walls and galloped through the castle grounds. Snorting and tossing their manes and tails, they circled the same way the Shades had circled. Round and round they galloped, faster and faster until they became a pure white blur.

They herded the Shades into the center.

Myrddin raised his staff and his voice. "Shades," he called, "Doona and Cullyn have entered the Mists. Your time of bondage is over. You are free once again to make a choice."

The galloping slowed and stopped. The Shades, eyes glittering, nervously looked at Myrddin and the other Wise Ones, all pointing toward the magical doorways.

"You became Doona's Shades because you lacked the courage to enter the Mists when your life was stripped from you," continued Myrddin. "Dark and Light, Light and Dark. The choice is offered again. There is also a third choice. The Cabbyl Ushtey, the magical water horses of Gaia offer chance of a new life. Those of you who still cannot bear to enter the Mists may climb on their backs and find sanctuary in the realm beneath the sea. Your belief in them will strengthen the Cabbyl Ushtey and halt their fading from Gaia."

Runesong stirred a puff of luminous mist through the doorway of light.

The nearest Shade glided toward it, paused a moment and passed through.

A silent whirl of movement followed.

"Some are choosing the Dark," whispered Owen in disbelief.

Chantel's eyes pooled with tears. She huddled against Adam. He hugged her tightly as they watched the Shades make their choices, and the Cabbyl Ushtey, many with dark riders, gallop back to the waves.

<hr />

The sunset was magnificent.

The townspeople, their disagreements forgotten, lingered on Peel beach, celebrating its beauty and discussing the unexpected eclipse.

No one noticed the more somber party gathered at the top of the round tower.

Adam sat on the stone flags, one arm around Chantel

who clutched his hand as though she was never going to let him go.

Owen leaned against Equus and gently stroked Ava who perched on his arm in her guise of a small hawk.

Manannan had fetched Mr. Smythe and Mr. Cubbon, and he and Myrddin talked quietly with them.

Only Holly stood apart, the magnificent necklace still around her neck. Lips parted in a tiny smile, she stared as the sunset cast its golden light across the sea, stared as though she had never seen a more beautiful sight.

She hadn't. Each stone in the necklace tugged at her inner vision. Her eyes saw past Gaia's familiar sun, to undreamed of stars and planets, all sharing their light, calling, beckoning and singing a welcome to her.

Owen cleared his throat. "Put us out of our misery, Sis. What are you going to do with the necklace?"

Everyone held their breath.

Holly came back to earth. She laughed and lifted the beads over her head. She held the fabulous links up for everyone to witness and sighed. "It's so very beautiful," she said. "I wish it were mine."

Then she snapped the hair and let the beads run off into her pocket. "We'll put them back in the archaeologists' tray before we leave." She dropped the hair over the parapet.

"But...but no one will know what order they should be in," stuttered Owen.

"That's right," said Holly, watching the hair drift away. "It isn't our magic. This way, it never will be our war."

EPILOGUE

The Land Rover turned into the yard of White Horse Farm and tooted its horn.

Ron Maxwell appeared at the doorway. "The kids are back," he called.

Lynne joined him.

The four children hung out of the car windows, waving madly.

"Who's the visitor?" said Holly as another figure appeared behind them.

"DAD!" yelled Adam and Chantel. They tumbled out of the car into his arms.

Explanations from the children were surprisingly easy.

Descriptions of Glastonbury Tor and the labyrinth, and runes and ruins seen during a twenty-four-hour trip to the Isle of Man, more than satisfied the adults that the cousins had experienced an exceptional trip.

Mr. Smythe was invited to stay for tea.

The children unloaded their backpacks and carried them up to the bedrooms.

Chantel sat at the top of the stairs and waited for Adam.

"I've something to tell you before we talk to Dad. Mom phoned while you were off in the mist."

Adam grunted. "Who did she trash this time?"

Chantel shook her head. "No one, but...," her eyes filled with tears, "...she said you would go to live with Dad, and I would live with her."

"WHAT?" Adam dropped down beside her. "You've gotta be kidding. No way are they going to split us up." He gave Chantel a massive hug that made her bones crack.

Chantel gasped, not knowing whether to laugh or cry. "You mean it, Adam? You really mean it? You don't think it's a good idea?" She gazed up at her older brother.

"Course not," said Adam gruffly. "Mom and Dad are divorcing, not us. We'll tell them."

"Mom won't listen," said Chantel sadly.

"We'll *make* her listen."

"How?" said Chantel. "We'd have to do something big, like running away."

"Can't do that," said Adam seriously. "I missed home like crazy when I was captured." He punched the air. "We'll go on strike?"

Chantel's eyes widened. "We will?"

Adam grinned. "We'll walk up and down in front of the house holding signs: *Cruelty to Kids*; *Don't split us up*. And we'll phone the TV news first, so they'll cover it."

"That would be sooo embarrassing," said Chantel doubtfully.

"Exactly!" said Adam. "Mom hates being embarrassed."

"We could refuse to go to school," Chantel said slowly.

"Refuse to do chores," added Adam.

"Go on a hunger strike," said Chantel.

There was a long pause. "Naw. No sense not eating," said Adam. "Got to have the energy to be obnoxious."

Chantel laughed.

Adam hugged her again. "We'll make them listen, Chantel. We'll keep telling them what Holly told Doona and the Lady. It's their divorce. It's not our war!"

"You're right, son. It's not your war."

Their father climbed the stairs and sat between them.

Chantel shot him a sideways look. "What did you hear?"

"Enough." He sighed. "We'll try to give you kids some choices, so you don't feel caught in the middle."

"Like what," Adam said suspiciously.

His dad shrugged. "Like how it's best to share you. We both want you. Can you live part-time with me and part-time with your mom? Lots of kids do that."

"Yeah, Colin Deskey does. One week with his mom and one week with his dad. He's always leaving stuff at the wrong house." Adam hunched his shoulders.

"Weekends with one parent, schooldays with the other?"

Adam shrugged.

"Or the school year with one parent and holidays with the other. That would allow one of us to try out a job in another place."

"Like where?"

"Like England. Uncle Ron needs a farm manager."

"England! More summers here?"

"Or school in England and summer in Canada. We'll look at all the options, and you'll have a say. I promise."

"You and Mom aren't going to get together again, are you?" said Chantel sadly.

"No," said her dad honestly. "But it's not your war."

※※※※※

When it was time to exercise the ponies, no one discussed the direction for the evening ride. They all knew.

"Everything started here," said Chantel as they reached the crest of White Horse Hill. "Where Equus first spoke to me."

"And you walked seven times around the eye of the chalk carving and found half his talisman," said Holly. She slipped off Harlequin and tied him to the fence.

"None of you believed me." Chantel giggled.

The four cousins walked to the ancient white chalk lines carved through the grass that gave the hill its name. They sat above the eye, looking out over the valley.

"What a summer. Totally unbelievable," said Adam. He chewed a clover head. "Do you think we'll hear from the Wise Ones again?"

"I think so," said Owen, "if we want to." He lay back on the grass and watched a hawk circling in the sky. "But more on our terms. As equals."

"So...did anyone actually win?" asked Adam.

We all won, replied Equus.

GLOSSARY

Bollan Bane—a herb still worn by the Manx on Tynwald Day to ward off evil.

Cabbyl Ushtey—(cavel ushta) the wild white horses of the sea that take riders below the waves. The riders can breathe if they are good; they drown if they are bad.

Cullyn—(coo-lin) archaic Manx for holly (modern Manx Gaelic uses *hollin*). I use it as a proper name to facilitate the story's plot, but it isn't used that way in the Isle of Man.

Isle of Man—a small island in the middle of the Irish Sea, between England and Ireland. Ancient name Mann, used here as an Old Magic name. Also affectionately known as Mona, or Ellan Vannin.

Lhiat myr hoiloo—(l'yat mer hohl-yu) an old Manx saying, meaning, "To thee as thou deservest."

Manannan—Manx Celtic Sea-God. His full name is Manannan Beg Mac y Leir, which translates as Lord of Mannin, son of the sea. His name has appeared through the ages as Manannin, Manannan, Mananan, Manan, Mannin. Currently on the Isle of Man it is spelled Manannan.

Manx—the term used for people born on the Isle of Man and their cultural traditions, folklore and language.

Manx cats—a breed of tailless cats indigenous to the Isle of Man.

Moddy Dhoo—(mawtha doo) Black Dog.

Paitchey—(pay-chee) child.

Paitchyn—(pay-chin) children.

Pheric—(feric) a boy's name. An early form of Patrick.

Runes—ancient Norse symbols comprised of straight lines that could be easily scratched into wood or stone. One of the earliest forms of accounting and writing. Some of the best surviving examples in the world are found on the Isle of Man.

Skeet—gossip, news.

Spooyt Vane—(spoot vairn) White Spout, the name of a waterfall in Glen Mooar said to have magical properties.

The Three Legs of Man—the island's national heraldic symbol, seen in the center of the Manx flag and found on many buildings. The three legs, clothed in armor and joined at the thigh, are one of the forms Manannan takes when under threat.

Tramman Tree—the Elder tree.

Author's Note

Behind the Sorcerer's Cloak is the culmination not only of the Summer of Magic Quartet, but of a life-long love affair with the Isle of Man.

From my first visit at a few months old, until I was twenty-one, I spent annual summer holidays on Ellan Vannin. I played in the ruins of her castles, sailed the surrounding waters and hiked the mountains, glens and beaches, sometimes with family, sometimes with Manx friends and sometimes on my own, for those were the days when children could safely wander without comment as long as they returned in time for meals.

My wanderings were always enlivened by daydreams, for on the island of my childhood, dreams and magic were a part of life. Folktales were still told and superstitions still acted upon. I cannot remember a time when I didn't know about Manannan, the Moddy Dhoo and the Cabbyl Ushtey, and to this day I see white horses in the crests of waves.

Manannan's presence on the Isle of Man is still acknowledged, and his "cloak of mist" is often drawn to hide the island from view. To the great delight of the Manx, this almost always happens when English royalty visits. The Manx are fiercely proud of the fact their island, though under the protection of the British Crown, has its own thousand-year-old parliament, Tynwald, and is not part of the United Kingdom. Manannan obviously agrees and continues to shield his island from British invaders.

Manannan is said to live on the summit of South Barrule where the remains of ancient walls and ditches of a

Bronze Age hilltop fort can be seen. I can no longer climb to the peak as I did in my youth. But last year my friend Nina sent me a photo of herself on the summit, placing a white quartz rock there for me. This Manx tradition of marking important places with white quartz has continued for centuries; I used the tradition to mark Breesha's grave in my story.

The burial of Breesha is based on what I know of the Pagan Lady's grave found within the walls of Peel Castle. She was buried over a thousand years ago, with a magnificent assortment of grave goods, including a necklace of colored glass and beads from around the world. Her necklace sparked my imagination and gave me the thread for the entire fantasy quartet. The necklace is on display in the Manx Museum in Douglas, though no one knows the real order of the beads.

The picturesque ruins of Peel Castle and the Round Tower on St. Patrick's Isle are tourist attractions and the highlight of a visit to the fishing village of Peel. But in my story I used "Pheric," the older Manx name for the isle.

Peel was home to the biggest herring fishing fleet on the Isle of Man and was once a center for smuggling. Countless stories are told of secret passages under St. Patrick's Isle and the town, though the only one I've seen is in the basement of a restaurant on the Nebb estuary, opposite the castle. The Castleview Inn and its secret passage to the Round Tower are figments of my imagination.

My center of research was the House of Manannan, a wonderfully imaginative interpretive center and museum in Peel, where I learned of early burial traditions and of the intermarriage between Manx women and Viking invaders. I used what I learned as the basis for the chapter about Breesha.

Several times over the last few years, my husband, David, and I revisited the island and looked at runic inscriptions, ancient settlement sites, magical glens and stone circles. One day our friends took us on the electric railway to the summit of Snaefell, the highest mountain. There I was able to survey the entire Kingdom of Mann, as Manannan does from Barrule.

This book reflects my fascination with Manx folklore and traditions. It was great fun to weave so many elements through my story!

Behind the Sorcerer's Cloak is set in real sites on the Isle of Man, but there reality stops. It is a fantasy story. The characters, the situations and my liberal interpretations of the history and folklore are totally fictitious.

Pictures of Peel Castle and The House of Manannan and historically accurate information about the Isle of Man can be found online at the Manx government's heritage website:
www.gov.im/mnh/heritage/museums/peelcastle.xml.

Slane lhiu,
Andrea Spalding
Pender Island, British Columbia

Acknowledgments

Grateful thanks to the many friends who helped with this book, particularly those in Ellan Vannin.

Graham and Margaret McFee, and Nina, Dermont and Joanna Shimmin enthusiastically hosted, walked, drove and explored the island with me, sent photos and DVDs and answered my many e-mail questions. I wish I could have used every site and story we explored, but there is enough left over for another book! Fenella Bazin shared Manx music and many tidbits of Manx heritage. Her description of the excavation of the Pagan Lady sparked the central motive for the story. Jennifer Kewley Draskau shared her knowledge and passion for the Manx language and enthusiasm for all things Manx. Any mistakes are mine, not theirs, and I beg everyone's indulgence for the things I changed to facilitate the story.

My husband Dave, as always, provided practical support with his library and amazing research skills, and both he and our daughters supplied unlimited moral support. Thanks to the Orca Pod, especially Maggie, who hung in for the duration of the mammoth journey, and to Martin Springett for his inspiring cover art.

Special acknowledgment to the House of Manannan and the Leece Museum in Peel and to the Manx Museum in Douglas, Isle of Man.

AɴᴅRᴇᴀ SᴘᴀʟᴅɪɴG has written many beloved books for children. She hails from England, where she was long steeped in ancient lore. The landscape of the Quartet is the landscape of Andrea's childhood. She and her husband, David, returned to England four times to research the four books of the series. *The White Horse Talisman* was nominated for the Silver Birch, Hackmatack and Manitoba Readers' Choice Awards. *Dance of the Stones* was also a Silver Birch nominee. *Heart of the Hill* left one of her four characters in grave danger. Andrea lives with David on Pender Island, British Columbia.

THE WHITE HORSE TALISMAN

The battle between good and evil plays itself out through four children, a mythical horse and an imprisoned dragon.

It was seven minutes after midnight on the seventh day. Whoooooooosh! *A flash of light streaked the sky. A shooting star touched a strange carving on the hillside, and a magical horse shook itself free of the chalk and rose to its feet. It was seven minutes after midnight on the seventh day of the seventh month. The only person watching was Chantel. No matter. It was enough. The summer of magic could begin.*

Chantel, Adam, Holly and Owen must help Equus, the great white horse, find his mate and foal and regain his magical talisman. But as the horse rises, so does the dragon. The age-old battle between good and evil threatens the bond between Chantel and Adam and endangers the quest. This is fantasy at its best, a story that raises hairs on the back of the neck and sends satisfying chills up and down the spine, a story that, while clearly drawn from the rich world of make believe, feels truer than true.

Dance of the Stones

**The four children from *The White Horse Talisman* seek Ava's
circlet, buried within the ancient stone circle of Avebury.**

> *The third sunbeam shot its magical light into a valley.
> There towered a stone circle, great gray stones veiled
> in morning mist. The golden beam lit the dew-cov-
> ered grass. The tide of light flooded and washed each
> sarcenstone. The Stones were ready. As gray became
> gold, the largest stone spun on its axis, then stood sen-
> tinel as before. The dawn magic happened quickly,
> without witness. That was to change. Four ordinary
> children were about to be called to The Circle.*

Chantel, Adam, Holly and Owen are eager to begin the next stage
of their adventure. "The Stones have stirred," Ava, Hawkwoman
and Wise One, tells Owen, "The time is near for the Circle Dance."
The stones are the ancient stone circle of Avebury in England. But
the Dark Being approaches, and her servant, a wraith, blocks the
children's progress. When Ava is hurt, the children are thrown back
on their own resources. They must discover the ritual that will
release the circlet. Each child has a part to play in finding the circlet
and holding back the Dark Being.

BOOK THREE
THE SUMMER OF MAGIC QUARTET

HEART OF THE HILL

With the help of the other Magic Children, Adam seeks to retrieve Myrddin's staff, hidden deep within Glastonbury Tor.

Moonbeam by moonbeam the Tor drank in the magic,
until its crystal heart beat strong and the forgotten edges
of the ancient Labyrinth that climbed its slopes glowed.
Still the moonlight poured down. The Tor drank till
it could drink no more. Three large, white, oval stones
on its flanks shone with an inner radiance. Two stones
marked the entrance to the forgotten spiral path. The
third gleamed like an eye, high on the Tor's flank at the
path's goal.

In Book Three of The Summer of Magic Quartet, Adam's turn to lead the adventure has arrived. The Wise One, Myrddin, needs Adam to retrieve his staff from the Crystal Cave deep inside Glastonbury Tor. The quest grows more dangerous, however, and fear rises. Equus and Ava are far away, the Lady will not wake and Myrrdin is in human guise, unable to use magic without alerting the Dark Being. The four children are on their own. And as the Dark Being approaches, the children discover that danger can find them even in their dreams.